THE TYCOON'S SECRET CHILD

CINDY REDDING

CHAPTER 1

*L*eonardo Vitale woke up to the ringing of his personal cell phone. The woman in the bed next to him, her sleek naked body exposed to his view, mumbled in her seductive British accent, "Who is bothering you at this time of the night?"

"Shh, go back to sleep, darling."

On the second ring, she groaned and buried her head under her white satin-covered pillow.

Leonardo uncurled his arm from around her waist and rolled over. He reached past the empty crystal brandy glass to snatch his cell phone from the polished mahogany night table. Few people had access to his personal cell phone number. The screen displayed an unfamiliar number. "Who is this?" he snapped in his Italian accent.

"Mr. Vitale, my name is Jessica York. You don't know me. I'm with Texas Child Protective Services. We have your daughter here."

"You are mistaken. I don't have a daughter." His thumb slid across the glass screen, and he ended the call.

Before he could place his cell phone back on the nightstand, it rang again. The woman next to him groaned. He growled into his cell, "Stop calling."

"Miss Rose Steele is the child's mother, Mr. Vitale, and our office was informed that you are the little girl's father."

Leonardo's black brows shot up; now he was fully awake. He pushed himself to sit up on the massive bed. The woman on the other end of the call sounded unruffled and would not take no for an answer. He knew this from years of negotiating experience as head of a multi-billion-dollar business. He threw his long, muscular legs over the side of the four-poster bed and stood. Leonardo strode over to where his pants laid neatly folded over the back of an apple-green, watered-silk bedside chair. "One moment, Ms. York," he said in a hushed tone. Leonardo glanced at the woman asleep in his bed, her head under the pillow. Her blond hair brushed the top of soft, fair-skin shoulders. He turned and walked barefoot across the warm wood floor into the other room. He turned the dial on a wall switch, and his study filled with muted light. Leonardo gently closed the connecting door before he demanded, "Why are you calling me?" He sat on his leather desk chair and listened.

"Mr. Vitale, Rose Steele was the victim of a hit and run. She is unconscious and is in the hospital. You are the only relative we have been able to locate. You're listed as the father on the child's birth certificate."

Leonardo ran his fingers through his black hair. "What hospital? When did this happen?" he snapped. *Rose, Rose, please be all right.*

"I'm not at liberty to say more than she is at Houston General, and Isabella is in our custody."

Isabella, my mother's name. She named her little girl after my mother. "I will be at your office in the morning. Text me your exact address."

Leonardo ended the call with Miss York and called Joe

Alberti, his lead personal assistant. Leonardo Vitale employed four personal assistants, and Joe oversaw all of them. Yes, it was two a.m. in London—but that didn't matter.

"Yes, sir?" His PA sounded groggy.

Leonardo wasted no time. "Wake my pilot. Have him file a flight plan to Houston, Texas. We leave immediately. Call Frank, have him pull whatever strings are necessary. I want to know every detail of Rose Steele, her life from the moment—*from three years ago, when she walked out on me,* in Naples to now. I want to know everything. And Joe, I know you remember Miss Steele, but Frank Coletto didn't work for me then, so make sure that when Frank thinks he has all the information, have him search further. Tell him not to leave anything out. Understood? I want both of you with me in Texas. We may need a nurse for Rose and a nanny for her little girl. Have that all arranged before we land."

Leonardo ended the call to his PA and then proceeded to shower. He dressed in black trousers and pulled a black cashmere turtleneck sweater over his head of blue-black hair. He slipped his feet into custom-made Italian leather loafers and went into his bedroom to wake up his fiancée Caryn Richards.

"Hmm, Leo," she said in a sleep-filled voice. Her arm came around his neck. She opened her eyes. "Why are you dressed in the middle of the night? That call you received, is everything all right? Is it your grandmother?"

"No, it's not my grandmother. She's fine as far as I know. Nothing to concern yourself with, darling. I have to go. I'm not sure when I'll return to London."

He could hear the concern in her voice. "Call me as soon as you can. I'm meeting with the wedding planner on Tuesday... I thought you'd be here to go over some of the details."

He brushed his lips along her sleep-warm cheek. "We can video chat."

It wasn't unusual for Leonardo to be gone for weeks on end. He owned a chain of luxury hotels that catered to the ultra-rich. Royalty and heads of state from around the world frequented his properties. Along with the hotels, he owned clubs, discreet clubs that again catered to the rich and famous. He could be in Asia for breakfast, the Middle East for lunch, and home in Italy for dinner. "I don't know when I'll return. You know how hectic my schedule is with the hotel renovations and the new hotel I'm building." He ran his thumb along her lower lip. "You know you can do whatever you want. You have carte blanche." Leonardo pressed a kiss to her soft lips. He grinned and said, "Just let me know, morning suit or tuxedo." He brushed another kiss over her lips and ran his hand over her naked backside before he pulled the apple-green-and-gold-striped comforter from the foot of the bed to cover his fiancée.

Caryn could do whatever she wanted for their wedding. He'd bought her a ten-karat diamond ring, worth three million dollars, because that was the one she wanted. The media circus of a wedding was all her idea and again, what she wanted. He would have preferred simple and understated, maybe in the garden of his villa in Sicily or on a secluded beach somewhere. As long as his grandmother and the small amount of family he had were there, he'd be happy. Definitely some close friends, but not the mess Caryn planned. It promised to be better than a three-ring circus.

"Wait, what about the wedding bands? The jeweler will be over this afternoon."

He brushed her blond hair back from her face and ran his knuckle along her smooth cheek. "You choose the biggest and the best ring you want. You know I don't want to wear a wedding band." He kissed her and then said, "I really have to go."

Leonardo hurried down the steps of his London townhome. At the curb, his driver waited by the back passenger door of a silver Rolls Royce limousine. It didn't matter that it was now two thirty in the morning. His staff was always prepared at a moment's notice. "Hello, sir. I brought coffee for you," he said, as he swung the door open for Leonardo.

"Thanks, Jerome. Tomorrow, you'll be available to take Miss Richards wherever she wishes?"

"Oh, yes, sir. As always."

Leonardo hopped into the backseat. Jerome closed his door and hurried to the driver's seat.

The ride from Kensington to Heathrow at this time of the morning was quick. His driver drove the silver Rolls Royce onto the tarmac where Leonardo's private wide-body 747 jet waited for him. The engines hummed at the ready, and his pilot and co-pilot waited at the top of the extensive set of movable stairs. "Hello, Mr. Vitale. Wheels up whenever you are ready."

"Let's do this, Captain." Joe had texted that he and Frank Coletto, head of security and Leonardo's personal security guard when he traveled, had already boarded, along with the entire flight crew.

Leonardo walked through the cabin. One of the twelve flight attendants he employed approached. "Hello, Mr. Vitale, would you care for anything?"

"No, thank you. I'll be in my office." Leonardo opened the walnut panel door to his private office. He went straight to the liquor cabinet and poured himself a whiskey from the crystal decanter. He toed off his shoes and sat on the plush leather sofa. The jet sped down the runway, and he closed his eyes. *Rose... Rose, why didn't she let me know she had a baby? My daughter...* He sighed and poured himself another whiskey. He drank it down as quickly as the first, not even savoring the flavor of his favorite drink.

Halfway across the Atlantic, Frank Coletto came into his

office and closed the door behind him. Frank was the same height as Leonardo, with the same lean, muscular build. Frank was a NYPD captain when Leonardo asked him to join his staff. Now, Leonardo motioned Frank to take a seat. "Hey, boss, it's pretty intense, although nothing unusual or shady. Three and a half years ago, Rose Steele was an archeology major, studying for her master's degree in Italy, at Pompeii to be exact... But I guess you know that. Your name popped up right away when I began my search."

Leonardo nodded and waved him on. "I know. Get to the important stuff. When was the baby born?"

Frank thumbed open a blue manilla folder and handed Leonardo a photo. His eyes widened, and he held back a gasp. A little girl with black hair curling around her tiny shoulders and deep blue eyes with a great big smile stared back at him. She had Rose's fair complexion, but his hair color and his exact eye color. This was his daughter.

"Oh yeah, then three years ago, Rose went back to the States suddenly, without warning, on the last day of her final dig. She just left. She had more than enough credits. Her thesis was about complete, so she could receive her master's degree the following January."

"Get to the child." Leonardo said, striving for patience.

"Yes, well, she was pregnant and needed to get home, find employment..." Frank looked up.

Leonardo stared into the brown eyes of his bodyguard. One brow rose in exasperation. "Go on."

"Well, she landed a teaching position at a community college in Houston. She'd have benefits and time to take care of the baby."

"Frank," Leonardo growled between gritted teeth.

"Okay, boss. Well. she hired a sitter to take care of the little girl in the evenings... by the way, you're listed as the father. About two weeks ago, Rose was working late, teaching an evening class. When she left the campus, walking the few short streets to her apartment, a drunk driver hopped the curb and hit her from behind. He never stopped, but the cops found him through surveillance tapes and arrested him. He pleaded guilty at his arraignment and will be sentenced next week."

Leonardo came forward on the couch and slammed his open hand on the coffee table. "Why is it so difficult for you to tell me what you've learned about Rose?" His voice boomed through the office.

"Sorry, she was badly hurt and… lay unconscious in the bushes near where she'd been hit. It wasn't until the next morning when some kids were going to class and found her… almost dead… boss. She was taken to the hospital and put into a medically induced coma." Leonardo rubbed the back of his neck and swallowed the bile that rose in his throat.

"She's lucky to be alive. Some broken bones, ribs, but actually, her right leg and right arm took the worst of it. No spinal injury, just a concussion. The doctor's plan on waking her today and if all goes well, they can move her to rehab in a day or so. They placed the little girl into temporary foster care. A really nice family is taking care of her."

Leonardo stood and pinched the bridge of his nose. "Will Rose be all right? I want to talk with her doctors." *She has to be.*

"Joe was on the phone with the hospital about a half hour ago. HIPPA and all that, but he's working on that for you."

"Good, then get some rest. It's going to be a long day once we land. Are the doctors optimistic?"

"From the little Joe and I could gather, yes, they are."

Leonardo lay on the caramel-colored couch and closed his eyes. Visions of Rose flashed in his brain. Rose on the day they met, as she rushed through the lobby of his Naples hotel. Her blond ponytail swinging behind her. She wore a blue button-down blouse, jeans, and sneakers. She carried textbooks in the crook of her arm… Leonardo smiled. He'd been scheduled to stay at his flagship hotel in Rome, but after meeting Rose, he stayed on in Naples. Six glorious months, with his wild rose before it all came crashing down.

A memory of Rose when they made love for the first time filled his head. She was dangerous, the kind of woman a man could get lost in. And he had. *Why didn't she tell me she was pregnant? Is that why she left so suddenly?* He never doubted that Isabella was his.

He'd loved Rose Steele more than he thought possible to love anyone. The petite American archeology major who spoke fluent Italian had taken his breath away from the moment she plowed into him in the lobby of his Naples hotel. Now, Leonardo hid his worry behind a mask of indifference. *She had to live, be all right...* He'd never stopped loving her.

CHAPTER 2

Rose Steele heard the annoying beeping sounds from a monitor before she fully awoke. She stared into the eyes of a stranger in a white lab coat.

"Hello, Rose. I'm Doctor Smith. You've been in an accident. Try not to move too much. You've been in a coma for two weeks."

She was so groggy and unable to focus. Her brain was blank for a moment. *Accident? Coma?* Then she remembered the most important thing in her life. Her eyes rounded. She tried to sit up but couldn't. "Easy, Rose. No sudden moves. We have to go slow."

"Isabella," she croaked out, her voice barely a whisper. Her throat hurt. "What happened? My daughter, Isabella, where is she?" It was difficult to talk.

"She's fine and being well cared for. You need to rest and in a little while, we'll see about getting you out of bed." Doctor Smith slowly raised the head of her bed so that Rose could gradually sit up, taking in the track lighting and the coffee-colored walls. Beyond the partially open privacy curtain, a flat-screen TV hung on a wall near the ceiling. The beeping came from a monitor with a blood pressure cuff attached to her left arm. She glanced down to see she wore a yellow flower-print cotton hospital gown. Her right arm was in a cast and although a blanket covered her to the waist, she felt the heaviness of a cast on her right leg. Her long, blond hair was in a single braid with a yellow ribbon tied to the end and rested over one shoulder.

A nurse in bright pink scrubs handed Doctor Smith a cup with a spoon. He fed Rose a few ice chips. "How's that?"

"Nice, thank you." She pressed her fingertips to her lips. They felt dry.

The nurse said, "Here is a balm for you to use. It will help with the healing." Rose nodded.

"Would you like to try a few sips of water?" Dr. Smith asked, holding a plastic cup with a straw for her. "We'll see how you handle that. Maybe later some broth and jello."

"My arm?"

His eyes filled with compassion. "Broken in several places. Your right leg as well and three ribs."

"How is Isabella? She must be so frightened."

"I haven't met your little girl. I was told that the foster family taking care of her said she is adjusting very well."

Her belly cringed, thinking of her daughter and how frightened she must be.

Doctor Smith bent close to her to hear. She couldn't talk above a whisper. "Can Izzy come here?"

He frowned. "Well… there is someone here to see you right now, but then I want you to rest. We can decide if it's wise for your daughter to come to the hospital. Maybe when you're stronger and moved to rehab. I'll leave you with your guest." Doctor Smith pulled the cream-colored privacy curtain open, and he and the nurse left the room, the doctor closing the door behind him.

Rose turned her head. And that's when she saw him. "Leo." His name rushed out of her. He was more handsome now than three years ago when she'd walked out of the five-star restaurant and left him sitting at their dining table. Only now he looked worried and was that concern she saw etched in the angles of his face?

Dressed in a dark-grey custom-made suit that fit perfectly to his tall, broad-shouldered, masculine body. He came to the side of the bed. His white shirt brought out his olive complexion and around his neck, a blue-and-grey-striped tie. The blue of the tie was an exact match for his eyes.

"Yes, I'm here. You get well and don't worry about anything. Isabella will stay with me until you can manage. If you like, I will bring her to see you."

"How…"

"How did I find out? I received a call from Child Protective Services. All you need to know is that I've hired help to take care of both you and Isabella."

She was too weak to move, and her voice drifted. Her lids felt so heavy. They closed, and then she forced herself to open her eyes, to make sure he was really here. Rose looked into the deep blue eyes of the sexiest man alive, the man who broke her heart with his callous words.

"Rose, don't talk. Rest, and I will return later today. You need lots of rest if you want to recover. Sleep for now." He bent, and his full sculpted lips brushed against her brow.

She breathed in his fragrance and memories flooded her. Happy memories of Leonardo lying in bed naked just after they'd made love. Holding her in the circle of his strong, muscular arms. They spent hours making love, talking, and laughing. She dreamt of him more nights than not. Sadly, the dreams always ended with that last time she saw him in the restaurant. *I never want to marry or have children.* His words stung even now, three years later.

Rose had excused herself, pretending to need to use the restroom, and walked out of the luxurious restaurant and away from him. She held her head up, swallowed her tears, knowing she was pregnant, and he didn't want her or the baby they'd made. All of his lies of loving her, needing her, came back. She stopped herself from thinking about that. She tried to calm herself as much as possible under the crushing sadness that came over her.

LEO'S spicy scent mixed with virile man lingered in the air as Rose lay in the hospital bed. She thought back to the first time she'd met him. She'd arrived in Naples the day before, ready for orientation at the Archaeological Field School. She was excited to spend her last semester before receiving her master's degree, interning at one of the most famous digs in the world. Rushing through the luxurious hotel lobby, she ran into a brick wall. Her books and papers went flying in all directions. The wall had a deep, sexy voice, and she smelled his delicious scent before she lifted her gaze to stare into vibrant, deep blue eyes. He was so very tall, with broad shoulders and a narrow waist; he wore a grey suit with a crisp white shirt. Around his neck was a blue silk tie. His platinum tie clip matched his cuff links. His blue-black hair neatly trimmed, a lock of thick hair fell over his brow. She'd wanted desperately to push it back into place. "Oh, I'm terribly sorry. I wasn't looking—"

"No need to apologize," he said with a dreamy Italian accent. "It's entirely my fault." The corners of his eyes crinkled as he said, "I wasn't looking where I was standing."

Heat splashed across her cheeks. He'd bent to help her pick up her books and notes.

"My name is Leonardo Vitale," he'd said as he offered his hand to help her up. His fingers wrapped around hers, warm and strong. A jolt of electricity sizzled through her body, ending with a delicious pulsing between her legs. The zing of pleasure completely replaced her embarrassment with desire. *When oh when was the last time you had sex?* Her brain clamored.

She spoke in Italian, "Thank you, Mr. Vitale. My name is Rose Steele. I hate to be rude, but I'm late and must find a taxi."

"Allow me to take you wherever you wish."

"Oh no, I couldn't possibly. Just a taxi."

"Will you have dinner with me tonight?"

She couldn't help the smile she gave him. For the first time in her adult life, Rose wasn't sure what to say. *Yes, and then you can take me right to bed.* She'd chuckled. "I don't know you." *How lame is that?*

He'd held her gaze with his intense blue eyes. "Yes, you do… remember? Leonardo Vitale, we just met. My friends call me Leo," he'd said in his deep and dreamy voice. He cupped his chin and tapped his smooth, shaven cheek with his pointing finger. "Perhaps you need to know a little more about me." His dazzling smile took her breath away. The other people in the lobby melted away. His cologne wasn't overpowering, like some men. She couldn't stop herself from leaning in to sniff his wonderful scent. Could she buy a bottle of it to remember him by?

Then he said, "I'm thirty-six, not married or in a relationship. Right now, I'm staying here in Naples, although my home is in Sicily."

She smiled up at him before she said, "Okay, but I'll pick the place. I'm really going to be late." Rose slipped her phone from her pocket and handed it to Leonardo. "Give me your number, and I'll text you when I know better where I'll be."

He took the phone, his slim brown fingers tapping the screen as he entered his number. Then he gave her phone back to her. He walked her through the lobby and out into the early morning sunshine.

The doorman greeted him. "Mr. Vitale, a pleasure to see you."

"Hello, will you please call one of our hotel taxis for Miss Steele?"

"Taxi? Oh, yes, immediately, sir."

That's when she made the connection. Vitale Hotels. "Are you that Vitale?" she whispered.

He smiled, and she almost melted into a puddle at his feet. "Yes." he said in a hushed, sexy voice. A hotel limousine pulled up to the circular entry, and Leonardo held the door open for her. "It has been a pleasure, Ms. Steele." He kissed her hand. "Text me."

Too stunned to do more, she nodded, trying to get her heart rate to slow back to normal. He closed the limousine door for her. She told the driver where she needed to go. The dig at Pompeii.

That was three and a half years ago, and now here she is, lying in a hospital bed without her little girl. Had Leo met Isabella yet? What did he think? He'd come straight to the hospital after meeting the case worker. Izzy had his hair and eye color. An exact match of jet-black hair and deep blue eyes. She lay her head back against the pillow, and a tear slid down her cheek. She missed her little girl so much.

Leonardo came back to the hospital in the late afternoon. "Doctor Smith wants to keep you for observation. Just another day or so. I've reassured him that I will take care of everything. You can recuperate at my home in Sicily."

Rose sat forward in the hospital bed. "Leo, how is Izzy?"

As he smiled down at her, the corners of his eyes crinkled. "She's beautiful, just like her mother. Izzy knows she can see you in a day or so when you are discharged from the hospital. I went to her at the foster family and arranged to bring her to my suite later tonight. Unfortunately, the nanny I hired won't be arriving until tomorrow."

"Is she really okay?" Leo took Rose's good hand and squeezed her fingers, rubbing his thumb along her wrist.

"Once she learned she could see you soon, she started to play with her dolls. I don't want you to concern yourself. Just focus on getting better. He handed her a cell phone. "Use this for now. Look, the screensaver is a picture of Isabella." Rose glanced down at the phone and then smiled up at Leonardo.

"Thank you."

"Frank Coletto, my head of security, is working on getting your purse and belongings back from the police. I've hired a medical team, including a doctor and nurse, for the flight. Medical equipment has been ordered if necessary. We can fly to Sicily as soon as Dr. Smith discharges you."

"Is all that necessary? Why can't I stay here in Houston?"

"It will be better at my home in Sicily. I have everything you and Isabella will need. I have a well-equipped home gym, and if there is anything else you need, I'll get it. My entire staff will be at your disposal, and I can get to know Isabella… I haven't told her who I am… although the social worker mentioned it to her so that she would be more relaxed when I take her with me… She's calling me Daddy."

Rose sighed. "Are you good with that?" *You don't want children.*

"Yes, of course I am."

"Well, it's not how I wanted Isabella to find out, but I'm sure I can explain it to her once we are on the plane or in Sicily. Leo, do I really need a medical team for the flight?"

"Yes, your doctor recommended it, and I agree with him. It's a precaution, that's all."

"Okay, if Doctor Smith recommended it. How soon before they can discharge me?"

"He said he'd be by tomorrow morning. Once you're discharged, I'll come for you, and then we can get Isabella, so she isn't frightened."

CHAPTER 3

*L*eo watched Rose from under the fringe of his dark lashes. Seated in the back of his Rolls Royce limousine, she looked so frail that it frightened him. With Rose's permission, Frank Coletto had taken her nurse, Ms. Carrington, to Rose's one-bedroom apartment to get some of her clothes and a few of Izzy's toys. Leonardo instructed Frank to pay Rose's rent through the end of September and close the apartment.

He turned to Rose. She could barely sit up in the backseat of his limousine. Her right arm was in a cast and in a pink sling that held it against her tiny waist. Rose's right leg from her knee down to her foot was in another cast. His chest ached for her. Two weeks in a medically induced coma, she looked as if she'd lost a lot of weight. The casts would need to remain on for another three to four weeks. Dr. Smith had said, "The bones were knitting nicely." So that was good. He added that it would take time and proper nutrition to heal properly.

Rose was very pale, and her eyes looked sunken in — Her eye color had been one of the first things he'd noticed when they first met in Naples. As he'd steadied her, he felt the curves of her luscious body. He'd been hard the whole day just thinking about her breasts as the blue cotton fabric of her button-down blouse stretched across them and the gentle roundness of her hips in her jeans.

Then he'd noticed her unique eyes. The irises were two different colors. The inner ring by the pupil was brown with flecks of gold that spiked all around like a starburst, and the larger outer ring of the iris was green. Both eyes were identical, which was unusual and so unique. He'd learned that there was a specific name for that—heterochromia.

Now seated in the back of his limousine, Rose's clothes hung on her. Leonardo made a mental note to have his PA order a few outfits, some casual clothes, and some comfortable, stretchy clothes for her therapy sessions. He instructed Joe to have everything hanging in the master bedroom closet by the time they arrived at his villa in Sicily. He and Rose talked about how his home in Taormina would be the best place for her and his little girl to stay. The Sicilian sun could just about cure anything and definitely bring some color back into Rose's beautiful face.

Leonardo thought he'd never see her again, and now she would stay at his home, in the master suite. Not even Caryn had ever set foot in that house. She preferred the extravagant luxury of his hotels and their owners' suites with a personal chef and maids at her beck and call. She preferred that or his London townhouse in Kensington, which was more like a mansion.

Caryn loved London and Paris, but she tolerated Rome. Since their engagement was announced, the invitations poured in weekly, and his fiancée embraced the social life his prestigious name provided. She ordered couture clothes from all the top designers, as well as her favorite Birken bags, one in every color. Shoes for all occasions from the top designers in Europe. She sent him the bills. One day, soon after they announced their engagement, Joe had approached Leonardo on that. Leonardo had instructed him to pay for everything and whatever she wanted. "But sir, some of these items will take two to three years to be delivered."

"Just take care of it. Give her whatever she wants."

ROSE'S NURSE, Ms. Abigail Carrington, a middle-aged, highly competent woman with wheat-colored hair and chocolate-colored eyes climbed into the limousine and sat opposite her. "Hello, Miss Steele, Mr. Vitale."

"Hello." Rose said, and Leonardo nodded.

Leonardo patted Rose's hand. "I'll get Isabella. She's with her nanny and is excited to see you."

"I can't wait," she said. Rose sat eagerly, waiting to see Isabella for the first time since the accident. Leonardo emerged from his five-star hotel in Houston, holding Isabella's tiny hand. She was dressed in a pink frilly dress with matching pink bows in her black hair. She wore white ankle socks with lace ruffles and black patent leather Dior Mary-jane's. Leonardo carried his daughter's Disney Princess back-pack over his arm. He matched his steps to Izzy's smaller ones. Ms. Byrd, the nanny he hired, followed them.

Rose's nurse slid to the opposite side of the seat as Leonardo opened the back door.

"Mama, Mama, oh Mama, Izzy miss you." Isabella said as she threw herself onto Rose's lap. Her one good arm went around Isabella.

"Oh baby, I have missed you so very much." Tears trickled down her cheeks as she kissed Isabella.

"No go again," she said and hugged Rose's neck.

"I promise I won't." Rose kissed her daughter on the top of her head.

The nanny slipped into the car and sat next to the nurse. "Hello, Miss Steele, I'm happy to see you up." She'd met Ms. Sophie Byrd earlier this morning when the petite redhead came to her room at the hospital. They'd chatted about Isabella. She was impressed by Nanny B's credentials and happy that Leonardo had chosen Ms. Byrd.

"Thank you."

Leonardo climbed in and sat next to Rose. "Isabella, sit between Mommy and me, then I can get you buckled in."

He turned to Rose. "We'll be on the plane shortly. The medical staff is already on board. And you can rest in the bedroom until we arrive in Sicily."

It took an effort for her to smile at him. Last night in her hospital room, Leonardo had asked her doctor exactly what was on her mind. "When will Rose regain her strength?"

Doctor Smith had said, "Baby steps, Mr. Vitale, and Rose will improve. A good diet, fresh air, and rest. I 've spoken with the doctor you've retained in Sicily, and he knows the protocol."

A WHITE WIDE-BODY 747 sat on the tarmac, red and green stripes running the length of Leonardo's jet. His monogram LV boldly displayed on the tail. The Rolls Royce limousine glided to a stop at the red carpet, and Frank Coletto and the limousine driver stepped out of the car and opened the doors for the passengers. Leonardo unbuckled Isabella. "Will you walk with Nanny B while I help Mommy board the plane?"

She nodded her head vigorously. "Daddy, Izzy be good."

Leonardo ruffled her black hair, and then Nanny B stepped out of the car and waited for Isabella.

Rose's nurse stepped out of the other car door and came around to stand next to Leonardo. He waited for Rose. "Ms. Carrington, I'll help Ms. Steele board. You go make yourself comfortable."

Rose slid along the leather seat and swiveled before she swung her good leg, and then the one with the cast out of the car. She looked up at the mobile stairs covered in a red carpet leading to the entrance of the 747. Two men in uniform stood at the entry. *Can I climb up all those steps?* She sat with her shoulders slumped. *Where is my crutch?*

"Rose, let me help you."

She nodded, extending her hand to him. Leonardo enfolded her hand in his larger one for a moment, then turned it to kiss her palm. Thick black curling lashes rimmed his intent blue gaze. "I'm going to carry you."

"No, Leo, I want to walk as much as I can. Let my nurse help me."

He nodded. "Yes, but I'll help you." He extended his muscular forearm. "I think your crutch is already on the plane…My bad, I intended to carry you."

She couldn't help but roll her eyes at him. "I'm walking to the steps of the plane and then you can carry me… This is so much bigger than your other jet."

"I use this one for long trips. There are three bedrooms on board, so you can sleep all the way to Sicily. The medical team you met earlier today is already on board and will be nearby at all times." He flashed his brilliant smile, the one that always melted her. "You'll be trapped on my plane."

She ignored his comment. "Thank you for doing this, Leonardo."

They reached the mobile steps, and he slipped one muscle-covered arm under her knees and scooped her up. She hooked her good arm around his neck. His wonderfully delicious scent replaced the smell of jet fuel as it drifted around her. In her exhaustion, she leaned her head on his broad shoulder. Rose tried to forget he was engaged to another woman. She wouldn't let Leonardo know she followed him in the papers and magazines. Any chance she had to read about him and gaze at photos of him.

When she saw his engagement photo, a lump formed in her throat and stayed there for a week. The sleek blonde with her fashionable blunt-cut bob stood in a red-sequin Valentino gown that clung to her body as if it were painted on. She draped herself onto Leonardo, looping her arm through his in the photo and proudly displayed her left hand and the enormous diamond ring. *He didn't want marriage or children with me. Now he would have both. Am I making a mistake going to Sicily with him? Exposing my vulnerability over his rejection of me to him.*

If she stayed in Texas and went to rehab, then there would be no one to take care of Isabella other than keeping her in temporary foster care, possibly moving from one temporary family to another. That would be so confusing for her little girl.

Rose knew all too well how that was, having grown up in foster care. Luckily, with one loving family. They'd passed away just before she received her undergraduate degree. They'd left her a nice inheritance. The money was more than enough to pay for graduate school and have a small nest egg.

Did she really want to keep Isabella in foster care while Leonardo, her biological father, stepped up and was willing to take care of both of them? A nurse for her and a nanny for Izzy.

Leo was dressed in custom-made slacks that outlined a lean waist and his long, muscular legs. Even his shirts were custom made, this one in pale blue and of the finest fabric money could buy. His suit jacket outlined his athletic physique, but no tie. That was casual for the hotel tycoon.

Leonardo carried her up the steps and through the main cabin, past rows of caramel-colored, butter-soft leather recliners. Each seat had a large throw pillow in a brown and cream check pattern. He carried her into a bedroom with a queen-size bed, a night table, and a sofa with a coffee table and two reclining chairs similar to the ones in the main cabin. The silk shades over the jet's windows were lowered.

"When Isabella gets tired, she can sleep here with you. I'll stay on the sofa, so she won't be frightened."

Leonardo sat Rose on the bed, and she had a hard time letting go of him. She still loved him after all this time… his memory haunted her. His kisses and lovemaking she could never forget, and now they would be together at least while she recuperated. He'd never mentioned that he had a fiancée, and Rose didn't want to bring that subject up. *Let him tell me about her. What must she think of this?*

His deep, husky voice brought her back to the present. "I'll send the doctor and your nurse in. I think he wants to check your vitals."

"Again? They did all that before they discharged me today. I'm really feeling good, just tired."

"Then Ms. Carrington can help you get comfortable."

"It's really too much, the doctor, the nurses, all of this."

"Humor me." He brushed a slight kiss on her brow. "Once you're settled, you can rest."

"Thank you, Leo. Have I said thank you for all of this?"

"Yes, several times, but there is no need. I'll talk to my pilot and make sure we're ready."

Once the doctor took her vitals, he left, and Ms. Carrington came in with a small overnight bag. "Miss Steele, I think you'll be more comfortable in this nightgown. I brought your pain meds."

"Thanks, I'm tired, but not in any pain, so no meds. I think I'll try to sleep. Maybe later I can sit up."

"That's a good idea. I'll be right outside your door if you need me."

"It's a long flight. Why don't you go rest as well? There's a phone here, and I can call if I need you."

"Okay. Mr. Vitale gave me the bedroom next to this one. I think I will make use of it."

Rose lay her head on the pillow and pulled the caramel-colored satin comforter over her shoulder. She was asleep even before they taxied down the runway. She woke up with Isabella lying in the half circle of her good arm. Glancing around the luxurious jet's bedroom, Rose found Leonardo sitting in a recliner, his black-rimmed glasses on and a packet of papers hung from his long, lean fingers.

"Hi," she said.

"Hi, yourself." His smile dazzled her, and she felt dizzy with excitement. "We should land at the Vincenzo Bellini airport in Catania shortly. I have my helicopter waiting to take us to my villa in Taormina."

"Yes, your home. Thank you for doing this for Izzy and me."

"You just focus all your strength on getting better." He kissed her brow. "I'm going to make sure everything is ready for when we land."

Isabella snuggled closer to Rose and sighed in her sleep. "Mama." A short time later, her nurse and Isabella's nanny entered the bedroom. "Mr. Vitale said we'll be landing in about thirty minutes. Allow me to help you dress."

THE HELICOPTER SAT on a pad at the airport, with Leonardo's monogram proudly displayed on the body. Rose remembered when Leonardo had purchased the twenty-seven-million-dollar ride. The ten-passenger extravaganza had leather seats, walnut tables, and cabinets, even a small kitchen. She couldn't believe that. The windows were covered with silk curtains that could be tied back. 'Let's take it for a spin,' he'd said. They'd gone to Capri for a long weekend after he purchased it.

The helicopter was quick and efficient, landing on its own helipad close to Leonardo's villa. Cypress trees stood tall on either side of the wide walkway. Rose caught her breath as Leonardo's home came into view. The stone villa was tucked into the side of a hill overlooking the Ionian Sea. Spread out along the rocky terrain, prickly pear cactus flowered at this time of year, preparing to grow the rich fruit from summer to winter. Lavender and rosemary grew wild between the dwarf palm trees. Purple bougainvillea climbed up the side of the single-story villa.

The path to the front door lined with potted flowers, plumeria, roses, red carnations, and gardenia blossoms smelled wonderful as they perfumed the air. Rose insisted on walking once they reached more level ground. She'd never been here. Leonardo talked about his home often and always wanted to bring her to Sicily. He wanted to show her his villa and the beautiful island where he grew up. He'd wanted her to meet his grandmother Lidia Vitale.

She and Leonardo had spent their time in Pompeii at the dig or traveling near Naples and Rome. They'd drive in his Lamborghini along the Amalfi Coast down to Calabria near the Strait of Messina.

That one time they flew to Capri on his new helicopter. She'd fallen in love with the island of Capri. They never went to Sicily, and she never met his grandmother before everything changed, and she walked out on Leonardo.

Rose loved all of Italy. To her, it was an open-air museum waiting for her to explore. She loved the antiquities and unearthing the past, piecing together the ancient civilizations. Her friend Joan Davenport was an underwater archaeologist and right now was working in Calabria. They'd met while she and Joan were in Naples, studying for their master's degree.

Once Rose gained her strength back and the casts were off, she would like to visit Joan with Izzy before they went back to Texas. The director of the Pompeii archeological studies is from Sicily, and he'd always said that Italy was the garden of the world, and Sicily was Italy's garden. From the little bit she saw, she could understand why he felt that way.

Leo had surprised Rose when he suggested she recuperate here at his home and that he would transform his gym into a personal rehabilitation center for her. She'd wondered what his fiancée thought of that.

This was better than a hotel but living in one of Leonardo's hotels would have also been like living in a mansion. The suite of rooms he'd given her—in his home included three bedrooms, each with its own bath. Leonardo had hired an interior designer for Isabella's bedroom and had the room decorated for a little princess. A white-iron bed with a pink canopy covered in miles and miles of pink tulle cascaded to the floor. Painted furniture included a child-size table and chairs and a toy box overflowing with toys. A hutch with shelves of stuffed animals and story books. A fairy princess' room for Isabella. A small sitting room separated Isabella's room from the third bedroom. Rose's nurse and Isabella's nanny would share that room.

The largest bedroom included a separate sitting room and a sunroom. The sunroom was magnificent with three walls of floor-to-ceiling windows that could slide open. From there, she could walk out to a terrace. The terrace wrapped around the side of the villa and overlooked the infinity pool. The pathway to the pool was locked, and Isabella had strict orders not to go anywhere near the pool gate or further down the long, steep path to the private beach. "No, Mama, Izzy not go. You take Izzy when you better?"

"Yes, darling, we will go together once I'm better."

"Daddy come too?"

Leonardo walked into the sunroom just then. "Daddy, Daddy! Let's play."

"Okay. What would you like to play?" He glanced over at Rose. "How are you feeling today?"

"Tired but getting stronger. Not only from my accident but jet lag. It's only been a few days since we arrived. Maybe all the drugs from the hospital and my pain pills, I think as well. Your housekeeper Signora Santa Maria brought me coffee and an afternoon snack. Isabella too."

She jumped up and down, clapping her hands. "Milk and cookies."

"You did? What cookies did you have?"

"Izzy favorite, silly, chocolate chip."

Leonardo smiled at Isabella. "I like chocolate chip too."

Rose chuckled. She didn't think he'd ever eaten a chocolate chip cookie in his life. Hazelnut chocolate and raspberry, those were his favorites. He looked up at Rose from his crouched position, lifting Isabella in his arms. Her breath caught, and she had to remind herself to breathe. He looked like Adonis. She remembered his naked muscular body. The smattering of black hair on his chest and the way it narrowed to a thin line down his abdomen, his olive complexion, and black, wavy hair. Her fingers curled, wishing they could run through his hair and down his body, over his sculpted muscles. Excitement pulsed through her... *I have to get a grip.*

"Why don't you sit on the terrace?" he said. "You can get some well-needed fresh air while you read. Isabella and I can watch one of her favorite movies on her DVD player."

"Beauty Beast." Isabella said, clapping her hands.

"Yes, we'll watch *Beauty and the Beast*. You go to your room; do you think you can find the movie? I will be right there."

Isabella's black curls bounced on her head as she nodded. She didn't hesitate and ran into the adjoining bedroom.

Leonardo came over to Rose. "Do you want to sit in your wheelchair?"

She gazed into blue eyes, rimmed with black, thick, curling lashes. "Yes, will you help me stand?"

He did better, lifting her and helping her get comfortable in the motorized wheelchair. "Shade or sun?"

"Sun, then I can move into the shade if it gets too hot."

"Rose, I've delayed some business meetings and will fly to London in the morning, then on to Morocco before I return home. Maybe a week, two at the most."

"We'll be here when you get back." She smiled at him.

"Good, I'm happy to hear that. Can we have dinner together this evening?"

"In here, yes. I don't think I can be good company in the dining room."

"Perfect, I'll let the housekeeper know. Anything special you'd like for dinner?"

You, but you're engaged, and I don't cheat. When is he going to tell me? "Oh, I don't know. Everything is delicious. Surprise me."

"I know the perfect meal. I'll tell my chef personally. See you later," he said as he left the terrace.

THAT NIGHT, Rose chose a lilac cotton tiered dress with ties at the shoulders. Her nurse helped her into the dress that she'd found hanging in the walk-in closet, along with swimsuits, nightgowns, and frilly lingerie. Most of the dresses were casual, but some definitely for the evening.

Leo walked her out to the terrace where Signora Santa Maria had a damask-covered table with two upholstered dining chairs waiting for them.

The setting was too romantic for a couple that were no longer involved in a relationship. The housekeeper had placed tapered candles into an arrangement of fresh pink and white roses. Rose couldn't count all the tea lights that were scattered around the balcony. The scent of the melting wax and the fresh flowers drifted on the air. Leonardo's chef had made her favorite meal. *He remembered how much I love clams.* Pasta with fresh clam sauce. In Naples, she couldn't get enough of the clams and the delicate flavor. So much better than in the U.S. "You remembered," she said.

"How could I forget? At one point, I thought you would turn into a clam." He laughed.

Her gaze drifted to Leo's broad shoulders. His grey shirt, open at the collar, exposed his olive complexion where some of the black hair from his chest peeked out. Rose forced herself to gaze into his eyes. Then Leonardo handed her a piece of crusty Italian bread. Again, she marveled at how he remembered she loved the end piece of the bread. "Here, dunk the bread in the juice. Are you still on pain meds?"

"Yes, although much less, and I'm definitely weening myself off them."

He handed her a crystal stemmed glass. "Then here is some sparkling water with lemon. Once you are off the meds, we will celebrate."

"Thank you... I like that idea, Leo." She couldn't help but look at his chiseled features her gaze landed on his lips. The memory of those lips on hers and sliding over her body––

His lips pressed together, and he shook his head before he said, "Rose, I never thought to see you again... when you left me… at the restaurant…" He sighed. "I'm engaged to be married in a few months. Her name is Caryn Richards. She doesn't know about Isabella or you for that matter.… I never told her of our time together. I'm sorry I didn't tell you sooner, but it all happened so suddenly. The phone call from Child Protective Services, the hospital, all of it. I wanted you safe and cared for, and I want to get to know my daughter."

She didn't expect the knot of regret that settled in her stomach, so Rose hid her feelings behind a false smile. "I'm glad you finally told me." She took a breath and widened her smile, praying it would appear genuine. "I agreed to this because it's the best of both worlds. Leo, the only reason I'm here is so that you can get to know Isabella. Besides, you helping me is better than going to rehab. I get to stay with Izzy, and you get to bond with her."

"Yes, I suppose you're right." Leo walked her back to the sitting room in her bedroom. "I'll say good night now. I'm leaving for London tomorrow before breakfast. You may hear my helicopter taking off."

"Safe travels, Leo."

She watched his broad back as he walked from the room, closing the door behind him. The knot in her stomach grew, adding to the lump in her throat. Her eyes stung with unshed tears. *Did I expect it to hurt less, hearing about his fiancée from him? That he'd rather marry someone other than me.*

BEFORE DAWN, Leonardo flew to London. He had to see Caryn. When he arrived at his Kensington townhouse, Caryn was in bed, propped up against the pillows with a breakfast tray across her slender lap. She smiled up at him. "Hello, I'm so happy you're finally back. I missed you terribly."

He strode over to the bed and kissed Caryn on her cheek.

She wore a low-cut green satin nightgown, and the view of her high creamy breasts and cleavage did nothing for his libido. "How are you?" he said as he took a piece of toast from her plate.

"You haven't eaten? Let me call down for coffee. I know tea isn't your favorite."

"No, I had breakfast on my plane. I wanted a taste of the jam. Don't you know me at all?"

"Oh yes, sweets for breakfast with that strong espresso you like." She wrinkled her nose. Caryn handed him the breakfast tray, and Leonardo moved it to the sitting room, the signal to the staff not to disturb the occupants in the master bedroom. Leonardo tugged at his silk tie and unbuttoned the top three buttons on his custom-made shirt. He folded his suit jacket over the back of the bedside chair.

Caryn looked up at him and patted the bed. "I've made some plans for the wedding. While you were away, I finalized the menu for the pre-wedding ball."

Leonardo toed off his shoes and came to recline on the bed. His heart wasn't in this. While he flew to London from Sicily, he thought he would go through with the wedding. But at this moment, lying next to Caryn, he didn't think he could. Her beauty couldn't entice him. All he thought about was Rose and his daughter. It weighed on him that he was engaged and relieved that last night, before he left Rose, he'd finally told her he was engaged. The smile Rose had given him at his news hadn't reached her eyes. He thought about that all night.

And Caryn well, that was worse. He hadn't told her anything.

She rolled over into his arms. "I've missed you so much." She pressed her lips against his, and Leonardo knew he had to tell her right now about Isabella and Rose.

"Caryn—"

"Shh, no talking." She ran her hands along his abdomen, reaching for the zipper of his suit pants. "I'm so wet for you. As soon as you walked in, my body sprang to life."

He kissed her and dragged her across his lap so that she straddled him.

"Oh, yes." Caryn unbuckled his leather belt and slid the zip down. She slipped her hand into his silk boxers. Her touch did nothing to arouse him. She scooted off his lap and bent to use her mouth to excite him.

He'd never had such a reaction before. He was always ready. Closing his eyes, he cupped her head and concentrated on what her lips and tongue did to him.

She lifted herself and pulled off her nightgown before she straddled him. He closed his eyes, and it was Rose. *No!* His eyes popped opened, and he concentrated on Caryn. She kissed him as she rode him faster and faster. He was relieved when she rolled off him to lie against him before she fell asleep.

Leo silently got up and went to take a shower. Feelings that he didn't want to face surfaced. Rose left him; he didn't leave her. He'd loved her and if he were honest with himself, he loved her still. Leonardo had to tell Caryn. By the time he dressed in another suit, she awoke. He asked her to sit in the sitting room so they could talk.

Caryn seemed to take it in stride, telling him they'd work it out, and she understood after all, he had a life before they met.

That night, again, he had to force himself to have sex with her. She asked him what was wrong. He said he was tired, but he was torn. He had to be blunt with her. How could he when he didn't even know himself what his feelings were?

When he left London, Leo went to France to see his mistress, thinking that would help his mood, but he couldn't make love with her either. Years of his mother telling him he was just like his father pounded into his head. He believed her because it was his father's blood running through his veins, that "sex with anyone" attitude, but he had lost all desire for his fiancée and the brunette model. He knew how to make money like his father, but he wasn't into drugs and prostitutes like him, or a womanizer for that matter. Once he fell in love, he was committed.

He flew to Morocco for a meeting with his general manager. The hotel in Marrakesh needed some major improvements, and he wanted to see firsthand what that would entail. He had to stay longer than he planned, and Caryn surprised him, coming to stay with him for a few days. Then he flew to Rabat to talk with the prime minister about another project he was interested in purchasing.

Leonardo decided he had to confront Rose. Thinking of making love with Rose filled him with a desire that had never ended, even when she'd left him. When he finished his business, he would return home, and he had to talk to her and get the matter straightened out.

Rose sat in her ergonomic power wheelchair taking in the breathtaking view from the living room. The lush Mediterranean garden bloomed with lavender, rosemary, and a variety of plants. Mosaics hung on a wall and in the center, a fountain gurgled. The stone walkway through the garden led to an overview of the sea beyond. Once her casts were removed, she'd go for a walk through the garden. At the sound of footsteps, Rose pressed the joystick and turned her wheelchair to face the arched entry.

Caryn Richards arrived in a swoosh of activity, snapping orders at the staff. "Get my room ready. Prepare me a bath. I'll have a light snack in the master bedroom and dinner in the main dining room."

She definitely looks every bit like the spoiled debutant she is. Tall and super thin with legs that seemed to never end encased in the latest fashionable white wide-leg linen pants. Her blond hair brushed her shoulders, the perfect amount of blush on her cheeks. She wore red-soled stiletto sandals, and her green silk blouse alone must have cost as much as Rose made in a month. Caryn waved her hand through the air, and her ten-karat diamond engagement ring made a prism of colors on the marble floor and nearby wall.

"Leonardo isn't here. He left on a business trip two days ago," Rose said.

"I'm aware, at all times, where my fiancé is. I'm here to meet you and your precious little one." Caryn turned to the maid. "Why are you standing here? Hurry up, get my room ready." She snapped her red nail-polished fingers in the woman's face.

Rose held her anger in check and spoke to the maid in flawless Italian. "She would like you to put her things in Mr. Vitale's room."

"Si, si. Subito." The maid bobbed her head and hurried from the room.

"So, you speak Italian. That's typical of Leo to find—well, never mind. Tell me where is darling Isabel?"

"It's Isabella, and she's napping." Rose fought to keep the irritation from her voice.

"Good, that will give us an opportunity to have a pleasant chat."

"I don't know what you think I have to discuss with you. The only reason I'm here is to recuperate from my injuries and for Leonardo to bond with his daughter."

"Precisely what we need to talk about. I'm his fiancée—"

"I'm aware of that." *How many times did she have to rub it in my face?*

"Leonardo was in London yesterday and not at all his usual self. He was preoccupied, and I'm a little concerned by his behavior."

Rose didn't want to talk about Leonardo with his fiancée. "I'm sure you will both work out your difficulties. If you'll excuse me, I have to meet my nurse for a therapy session."

"I had hoped we could chat about Leo. Why did you break up?"

Rose turned in her wheelchair. "You will have to discuss that with him. If you're concerned about me and Isabella being here, you don't need to. Just remember, you have his ring and soon his name. He never wanted to marry me and to put your mind at ease, I don't want to marry him, so there's nothing to discuss." Rose nudged the joystick, inching the chair toward the entry.

"Let me be the judge of that—"

"Mama, Mama." Isabella skipped into the room holding one of her stuffed animals, with Nanny B following her.

"Well, hello, aren't you precious," Caryn said as she bent from the waist to Isabella. Resting her hands on her knees, she said, "She is definitely Leo's daughter, with her hair and eye color."

Isabella was always friendly, but this time, she hugged her teddy to her and hid behind her nanny, choosing to stay away from Caryn.

"You'll have to excuse me. I must get to my therapy session. Isabella, would you like to ride with Mommy on her wheelchair?"

Nanny B helped Isabella onto her lap. The motorized wheelchair Leonardo had ordered for her was lightweight and a pretty purple color. It helped her out immensely. Isabella liked to sit on her lap, and they would scoot around the villa, laughing and singing nursery rhymes as they went.

Rose left Caryn in the living room. Signora Santa Maria said that Miss Richards didn't stay long after that. Rose got the feeling Caryn was uncomfortable in Leonardo's home. The housekeeper said that this was the first time Miss Richards had ever been in his home. She found that difficult to believe the way Caryn walked around the place.

After meeting Caryn, she was determined to get better as

fast as possible. She asked her nurse if she could increase the repetitions to her exercises and, with her doctor's permission, they did just that.

Rose was happy that Izzy would get to know her father before they went back to Texas. Maybe Leonardo would visit them and be a part of Isabella's life growing up. Rose would really like that for her little girl. She would have eventually gotten around to telling him about Isabella, but his attitude about children had prevented her from letting him know. *I don't want to get married, and I never want children.* The words echoed in her head over and over again. Leonardo's rejection of her couldn't have been clearer.

WHILE LEONARDO WAS AWAY, he video chatted with Rose and Isabella daily. He loved to listen to Isabella tell him what fairy tale Rose read to her. A week later, while they spoke, she told him she'd begun therapy in earnest. Rose lifted her arm into the screen's view.

"Look, no cast. Same with the leg. My doctor removed the casts today." She was getting stronger, and the calcium-rich food his chef included with her meals helped. The stiffness remained and her doctor recommended some therapeutic massages. She leaned heavily on her crutches, but she gradually began walking longer distances.

She said, "Izzy and I stroll around the pool and the gardens.

He couldn't keep the alarm from his voice. "Alone?"

"Of course not. Nanny B and my nurse come along."

"That's good. I'm stuck in Morocco for a while longer than expected. I may not call you for a few days."

"That's fine. I don't expect that, and Izzy is too young to notice."

"We'll talk when I get home. Kiss Izzy for me."

"Okay, Leo, we'll be here. Ciao."

LEONARDO DIDN'T WANT Rose to know that Caryn had joined him in Morocco. She showed up one day, saying that she missed him terribly. He spent his days with Joe and his team of attorneys in meetings and heavy negotiations for the new property he wanted to purchase. He avoided Caryn as much as possible. She lounged at their private pool during the day and ordered manicures and pedicures in their private suite. She'd have hair and makeup done every day and waited for him to return from his long days of meetings.

One night, she ordered a couple's massage for them. Rather than dinner in the owner's dining room suite after the massage, she ordered a light supper and then spent the night in his arms. On the third day, she announced she was going back to London. She had appointments with the wedding planner. Leonardo was relieved that he could once again focus on work and video chat with Rose and Izzy.

Another week went by before Leonardo could leave. He couldn't wait to see Rose and Isabella. When he arrived home, his housekeeper said that they were in the master bedroom, sitting room. He hurried straight down the hall, unloosening his tie as he went into the room.

The scene that greeted him filled him with a need to be a part of Rose and Isabella's life. Rose lay on a yoga mat, her blond hair in a messy bun, lifting one leg at a time, flexing and un-flexing her foot. He noticed she didn't wear nail polish and very little makeup. Isabella mimicked her on a much smaller mat. "That good, Mama. See Izzy?" They were in matching pink crop tops with turquoise cropped yoga pants.

"Yes, darling, you are such a big girl doing your stretches and such a big help to Mommy." She reached her hand out and pushed Izzy's black hair from her face.

"You better? Izzy get puppy now?"

Rose smiled at Isabella. "Oh… the puppy I promised you before my accident… Well, we may have to wait a little longer."

"Why?"

"Until we're back home, sweetie. Then Mommy will buy you the puppy you want."

"Why?"

Rose giggled, "Silly, it will be better once I can help you take care of a puppy. You know they are a big responsibility."

"Sponsily, why?" she said as she lifted her tiny leg and pointed her toes just like Rose.

"It means big girl things."

Isabella sighed. "Okay, Mama."

Rose rolled to her side and tickled Isabella, who giggled and squealed with laughter. Rose joined in, laughing along with her daughter.

Leo watched the adorable scene, and his heart twisted. He'd almost missed this and was about to make the biggest mistake of his life. He thought that marrying Caryn would make his grandmother happy. But what about him? He knew she wanted to see him settled down and have a family. God knew she had told him enough times. Caryn didn't want kids, and neither did he, but his grandmother didn't need to know that. Caryn was much more interested in keeping her sleek body than having children, and that benefited him.

He didn't want a wife either, but Caryn was a good choice. She would turn a blind eye to his affairs, and he would reciprocate in kind. She would be a marvelous hostess for his dinner parties and enhance his business meetings. Giving her whatever she wanted, including her subtle affairs.

As if I don't know she sleeps around. It gave him freedom to have his own affairs. Besides, he prided himself on not being jealous.

Leonardo stopped and ran his fingers through his hair before he took a deep breath. *I've turned into my father!* No, he didn't want to become the callous man his father was.

All of his father's dalliances and heartless behavior had hurt his mother. Leonardo remembered his mother's eyes and the look of sadness when his father didn't come home.

Once, when he was in his teens, he found his father at his newly opened club surrounded by women. He watched as, one by one, they went into the back office. Leo knew what went on there. Another time, his father pulled a waitress into his arms. Leonardo overheard his father say, "Come with me. I need to feed my dick into your mouth right now."

Leonardo was disgusted by his father's treatment of his employees. The waitress looked up, her eyes pleading with him, but he grabbed her and pulled her into his office. His treatment of women and the drugs he consumed—his father had become the lowest of humanity.

Leonardo didn't love Caryn, not the way he'd loved Rose, but the convenience of a marriage with her seemed right at the time. Now, he knew he couldn't marry her, not after seeing Rose again. Add Isabella to the equation, and all he wanted was them in his life. The shadow of a grin slowly turned into a smile as a vision of Rose surrounded by his children burst into his mind. In that moment, he knew without a doubt that he was nothing like his father. He'd never cheat on Rose... she was everything he could ever desire.

Rose struggled with her exercises, but that didn't prevent her from answering every single question Isabella had. He smiled as he watched Rose and his daughter. Leonardo wanted to be a part of this always. He wasn't around children much, but he realized that Rose never used baby words with Isabella. She patiently answered every one of his little girl's questions.

He walked into the sitting room. "Hello, how's my girl?" he said to Isabella, crouching down on his haunches.

Isabella jumped up from the purple yoga mat and ran into the circle of his outstretched arms. "Me help mama."

"I see that. You are such a big girl, helping." He turned to Rose. "How are you?"

"I'm much better."

"Tonight, will you have dinner with me?"

"Yes, I would like that."

His chef walked into the room holding two bowls filled with gelato. "Oh, Signore Vitale, I didn't know you returned. I bring a snack for *la piquella* Isabella," he said as he handed her a spoon and a small cup filled with chocolate gelato covered with sprinkles. Then he beamed a bright smile at Rose. "I make this special for you, Rosa, to help you heal."

"Thank you, Chef. You're too kind the way you always think of me." She smiled at him. Leonardo looked between Rose and his chef as a burning sensation gripped his chest. *What the hell is that? Anger, jealousy?* Whatever it was, he didn't like it. Then his chef turned to him. "Signore Vitale, would you like some gelato or a pastry, perhaps?"

"Yes, a pastry and some espresso, but bring it to my study."

"Si, right away."

Isabella stopped eating her gelato long enough to say bye to the chef as he left the room. Leonardo stayed for a few minutes and then, while Isabella had a nap, and Rose rested, he went to his study. Now that Rose was getting stronger, he had to talk with her about his grandmother coming over to meet them. He had neglected his grandmother and needed to let her know about Isabella.

Leo wanted an intimate dinner with Rose, so he waited for Isabella to go to sleep. Then he had dinner brought up to the terrace. Rose dressed in a casual light blue summer dress. She wore flat heel sandals. She'd tied her hair up in a high ponytail. Her blond hair made a thick curl at the end. She added eyeliner, making cat eyes, and she applied a barely there pink lipstick to her luscious lips.

He noticed that she'd begun using a cane for support. The wraparound terrace connected the master bedroom suite with the smaller one he'd moved into. It would be easier for her to get around, and they could enjoy the view. He led her out to where a table covered with a lemon-yellow tablecloth and two upholstered dining chairs had been set up for them.

The view of the sea and the coastline at dusk looked like a painting. The palm trees in the distance and the sandy beach along the coast laid out like a carpet. Homes and hotels climbing up the hill were all lit up in golds and pinks as the sky grew darker.

Once they sat at the table, Leo asked the question that had eaten at him since he saw her in the hospital in Texas. "Why did you leave me sitting in the restaurant?" He shrugged one shoulder. "You just left me there. You could have told me you were pregnant."

Rose lifted her gaze to him. "Frankly, I didn't want to stay around while you tried to turn what we had into a cheap affair. I was going to tell you that very night I was pregnant... I found out that morning... then you said you never wanted to marry or have children, so I left... Now, Leo, it seems perhaps... you didn't want to marry me as you're engaged. I met your fiancée Caryn, and she informed me of the huge wedding celebration you've planned."

It startled him. "She came here. When?"

"Two days after you left on your business trip. She stayed

less than a day and then went home, back to London, I guess."

Caryn had come here after I'd been in London. She despises Sicily. Then she met me in Morocco, but she never mentioned meeting Rose. He nodded. "Rose, that night in the restaurant, you misunderstood. I was trying to tell you I very much wanted to marry you. There was just so much of my father running through my blood, I wasn't sure that I wouldn't hurt you." He leaned forward. "It terrified me. I knew in my soul that I would be like him. After all, I'm his son in every other way, so why not his womanizing as well? I would never want that for you. To see you sad and hurt by my actions."

He sat back and took a long gulp of his red wine. "Maybe I would have mistresses the way my father did. I watched what he did and how it hurt my mother. He didn't care that she cried herself to sleep. He was downright mean, flaunting the other women in front of her. She died of a broken heart. There is no other way to put it. He hurt us both. I never wanted to have children, be a father like him, and hurt my child the way he hurt me."

His voice was full of disgust. He went on. "Choosing brief, meaningless affairs, or women for an hour or two, over his wife and child. This is what I was trying to say to you. I wanted very much to give it a go, a real chance at a marriage and a family with you. You were the only person who ever made me want those things. You are still the woman I love. The only woman I have ever wanted more with."

"Don't say that. You're engaged! Look, you're going to marry someone else… I will say that when I walked out on you… my hormones were already crazy and with the added pressure of my thesis and my degree, I just thought you were telling me you didn't want me."

"I have always wanted you… I have never stopped wanting you, Rose. In the beginning, I searched for you, but then when you left the country, I realized you didn't want me. After all, you left me sitting in a restaurant with no explanation."

I have to clear up this commitment with Caryn, and then I will have to —

"I'm happy we had this talk, Leo. I never believed you were anything like your father."

"You don't know."

Rose covered her heart with her hand and looked into Leo's eyes. "I know in my heart that you don't cheat."

Her words filled him with more love than he could ever believe possible.

CHAPTER 5

The following afternoon, Rose sat in the sunroom with Isabella. Isabella wore a Cinderella costume, right down to the imitation glass slippers that Leonardo had surprised her with. Rose read the fairy tale while Isabella pointed to the pictures.

"Princess."

"Yes, that's Cinderella."

"Like Izzy dress." Then her little finger glided along the glossy page to the illustration of Cinderella and Prince Charming. "You an Papa."

She looked at her daughter and smiled. "I guess with my hair color and Papa's black hair."

Leonardo walked into the sunroom holding a large square box wrapped in pink and yellow gift paper, a big violet colored bow in the middle of the cover. Rose looked at Leonardo. Her eyes narrowed, and her brows furrowed. Then she noticed holes were cut into the sides of the box.

"Isabella, I have a surprise for you," Leo said.

Isabella scooted off the sofa and scampered over to

Leonardo. "Me, me," she said with her little hands outstretched.

"Yes, but it's too big for you to hold." Leonardo placed the box on the marble floor as a little "Yip, yip," came from the box.

Isabella looked up at Leo, her eyes huge. He lifted the lid of the gift box. The cutest little puppy with a pink bow around its neck whimpered and scratched at the inside of the carton.

"Puppy," Isabella squealed as she clapped her hands.

Leonardo lifted the puppy out of the box, and Isabella sat on the floor, her little legs outstretched as her Cinderella dress pooled around her. The puppy ran into Izzy's lap and stood on its hind legs, its front paws on Izzy's chest, licking her daughter's face. Isabella giggled and hugged the tiny curly, black-haired dog.

Leonardo caught Rose's gaze and shrugged a broad shoulder as he tipped his head of black hair to one side. She smiled even though she shook her head and stopped herself from rolling her eyes at him.

His dark suit fit him perfectly, accenting broad shoulders and a narrow waist. "I couldn't help myself. I know it's a burden for you right now, but I've enlisted the help of Nanny B, and your nurse said she would also help. Besides, there's always one of the staff nearby until she's trained."

Rose couldn't help the smile that spread across her lips or the warm glow that went through her when she watched Leo and Isabella together. *How could he possibly think he's not a good father?*

A few days later, Rose rested in the sunroom with a full-leg ice pack wrapped around her leg while Leonardo worked in his study. She reclined on one of the two matching cream-colored sofas. A comfy pillow at her back, the view of the sea past the sun deck, winked at her like diamonds. The coffee table with its glass top was moved to a safer location so that Isabella would have plenty of room to play with her puppy. The three walls of floor-to-ceiling windows could slide open, bringing the outdoors in.

She'd finished a very grueling therapy session; her leg was improving, but she'd pushed herself so now, she rested while reading a book when Caryn walked into the sunroom. "We need to have a talk. Where is Isabel?"

Rose placed her book on the sofa next to her. "Oh, you're back. It's Isabella, and I believe that we have nothing to discuss."

"We most definitely do. Leonardo brought you here to his home for privacy and to help you recuperate. I understand that. He gave you the master suite... although that is confusing to me, I can certainly handle the situation. We are to be married in a few months."

This is his room! "Yes, I know he chose you." She tried and failed to keep the bitterness from her voice. "My daughter and I have a life in Texas. Once I can fully take care of myself, Isabella and I are going home. We will be gone well before your wedding. You have nothing to worry about from me." She lifted her book, dismissing Caryn.

Caryn didn't notice the subtle hint as she said, "Leo and I spoke about adopting Isabel once we're married."

She snapped the book closed and placed it back on the seat cushion next to her. *The utter gall of them discussing my daughter behind my back. Breathe, calm breaths, in and out. Stay calm.* Her eyes narrowed. "Did you now. Well, there's no way I would give up my child to you and Leonardo. Isabella is my daughter, and I have sole custody of her, and that is how it will always be."

"You should consider what is best for the child—"

Her fists clenched, and her stomach tightened. *The audacity of Leonardo and this... this... his fiancée to discuss adopting my daughter. The nerve of them!* "I am, and there will be no further discussion, because dear Caryn, if you haven't realized it yet." Rose paused, adding a firmness to her voice, she leaned forward before she said, "I, her mother, am what's best for Isabella."

At that moment, Isabella ran into the room chasing a little black fur ball. "Mama, Mama look."

The puppy stopped, sniffed a spot in the middle of the floor, squatted, and made a mess.

Caryn stood over the puddle that Isabella's puppy made on the marble floor. "This is disgusting and dangerous. Someone could slip on it."

Rose unwrapped the ice pack from her leg. Although Rose's leg was stiff from the exercises, she stood. Her leg ached from the workout, but not too bad. Taking a towel from the end table next to her, she walked over and laid it over the small puddle.

Caryn shouted, "That dog needs to be kept outside and not allowed in the house."

Isabella's chin quivered, and her bottom lip stuck out. She picked up her puppy and ran to Rose.

"No, Mama, mine puppy." Two fat tears hung on her lower lashes, ready to spill onto her soft pink cheeks. "Peeez, Mama." The tears rolled off her lashes and down her cheeks. The puppy licked Isabella's face.

Rose sat on the floor to hold her daughter and the puppy in her arms. There was no way she could get up from the floor, so she held her daughter and looked up at Caryn.

"You've upset my daughter. You have no right to dictate where the puppy stays. Now please leave."

Caryn's shrill voice pierced Rose's ears as she said, "I have every right as Leo's fiancée. Once we're married, all he owns will be mine as well. I want you, the brat, and that miserable dog out of my house."

Isabella wailed, "Puppy."

Leonardo rushed into the room, shirt sleeves rolled to his elbows, no tie, and his collar open. "What's going on here?"

"That mutt needs to be kept outside."

Leonardo hurried over to Rose. "You were trying to clean it up, Rose? You are still too weak. You've just recently had the casts removed." As he spoke, he scooped her up, along with Isabella and the puppy. Rose slipped her arms around her daughter and the puppy.

"Papa, mine puppy." Isabella had begun calling Leonardo Papa instead of Daddy.

"Don't worry, Izzy. Your puppy is safe. Would you like some milk and a cookie?" Leonardo turned to the maid, who had followed him in. "Please bring a tray with a glass of milk and chocolate chip cookies for Isabella and coffee for Rose, and a dog biscuit as well to Rose's bedroom. And send someone to clean this."

The maid hurried from the room.

He turned to Caryn. "We will talk shortly."

Once he walked from the sunroom and was down the hall, she said, "You can put me down now. I can manage."

"I like holding you in my arms with our daughter. You shouldn't have tried to bend or clean up the mess. You should have called someone to help."

"Well, your fiancée felt different. She upset Isabela, and I tried to comfort her."

Isabella whimpered, "Puppy."

"No one is going to take your puppy from you, Izzy. Have you picked a name yet?"

"Puppy."

Rose felt the vibration of Leo's chuckle against her breast, and her nipples tightened.

"That's good, but we will have to think of another name. Can I help you and Mama?"

"Yes, Papa."

"How about Lady? Just like the puppy in the movie we watched the other day."

"Oh, Izzy, Papa picked the perfect name."

"Lady. Yes," she said, hugging her puppy.

They reached the master bedroom. The door was open, so Leo walked in and helped Rose to sit on the king-size bed. Then Leonardo picked up Isabella and the puppy to stand near the bed. "The milk and cookies will be here soon. You play with the puppy until then."

Leonardo came back to her, and she looked up at him.

"I didn't expect Caryn to show up here today without calling." He ran his hand through his thick, black hair. "Look, Rose, I have no idea what you and Caryn talked about—"

"Oh really, you don't know?" she snarked. "Then let me fill you in. We talked about Izzy, adoption, me, your wedding, nothing earth shattering... I've been in this room for four weeks and didn't know that this is your bedroom." She glared at him. "We can stay in another room until Isabella and I go back home."

"I chose this suite for you." Leonardo's deep voice softened and reached through her anger. "I had my clothes removed to a different bedroom because the master suite afforded the most comfort for you. Izzy would be close to you. There is room for your nurse and the nanny... By the way, where are they?"

"After my therapy session, I gave them the afternoon off. They have been working 'round the clock, and I need to be more independent... take care of myself so that when Isabella and I go home, we won't need anyone."

"It will be awhile until you can go home."

She shifted her eyes toward Izzy. "We can talk later."

"Yes, tonight at dinner."

"Isabella and I will have dinner in here from now on. No need to get your fiancée's panties in a knot."

"Stop calling her that," he snapped.

"What am I supposed to call her?" She scowled at him.

"It's your tone that is irksome. Remember, you left me."

She crossed her arms over her chest. "Ugg, I don't want to talk about this now." Then she lifted her nose in the air. "Enjoy your time with your fiancée."

In a smooth, calm voice, he said, "It's okay. You and I will have all evening to talk... because Caryn is going back to London."

She snickered. "Does she know that?"

A ghost of a smile appeared on his handsome face. "She will very soon."

Her mouth dried, and her anger fled. She wanted to reach up and pull his head down to her. Kiss him and be kissed by him the way they used to. Where one kiss would lead to another and another before he would take her against the nearest wall, over the dining room table, in the shower, on his bed... He'd slip his finger into her as he kissed her to make sure she was ready—she was always ready—for him.

Now, he was engaged to a beautiful, statuesque blonde, and she turned away from him, getting her body under control. *What's my problem? He loves Caryn. I've never cheated in my life or thought of someone else's man. I won't start now!*

ONCE LEO SETTLED EVERYONE DOWN, and Isabella had dried her tears, he went back to the sunroom. Caryn sat on the sofa, her back straight, and her long legs rested to one side with her ankles crossed. She was turning her engagement ring around her finger. He sat near her on the opposite side of the sofa. *She's stunning, but not Rose. Let her down easy.*

"Caryn, this is not your fault, but I want to cancel our wedding—"

"Postpone the wedding? Why?" she shouted at him.

"No, not postpone. I no longer wish to marry. You should be free to find someone who will be devoted to you, love you, cherish you—"

"Oh my God, you're breaking our engagement, how could you? After all we've been through." She threw herself across the sofa at him, wrapping her arms around his neck, and Leonardo was disgusted with her *and* himself.

"Look, there is nothing between us anymore. You know that." He reached to untangle her arms from his neck. "You wanted to marry my name, and I wanted a safe haven and to make my grandmother happy, but love, you and I both know there was never any real love between us."

She looked up at him, her eyes blazed. "Of course there is. I gave you my virginity–"

He tried not to snicker and snorted instead. "Please, a thirty-five-year-old virgin. You and I both know that lame attempt at innocence wasn't lost on me."

She snapped at him, "Okay, so I wasn't a virgin, but you made a promise to me." Her voice rose an octave.

Leonardo knew she was right. "Yes, I did, and we will come to an agreement on the matter. The ring, all the other jewelry, the couture clothes you've ordered and the ones I've given you, the London townhouse, all the staff and a hefty monetary settlement so that we can end this charade."

She lifted her head and perked up. "How hefty?"

His voice held a chill as he said, "One hundred million dollars."

She smiled. "Four hundred million, and we have a deal."

He didn't argue. He wanted her out of his house and his life. "I'll have my attorney void the pre-nuptial and draw up the settlement papers for your signature. The money will be deposited in your bank account within the next several hours, and I would like you to leave here tonight." He stood.

"I'm happy to oblige. Let your flight crew know I'm leaving. Will Jerome continue as my chauffeur?"

"He's part of the staff in the London townhouse, and the Rolls is yours as well."

"Then we're done… it's settled. Neat and tidy. Can you have someone pack my bags and have your helicopter take me to the airport right away?"

"Yes. And Caryn, I wish you well. I hope you find someone who will love you and make you happy."

She stood and gave him a tight smile that looked more like a smirk. She turned and walked out of the room.

He breathed a sigh of relief before he walked back into his study. He called his personal attorney and told him what he wanted. Then he called Joe and made all the arrangements. He glanced at his wristwatch and then called Rose on the intercom.

"Please, you and Izzy have dinner without me. I'm busy this evening."

"Okay, Leonardo." She hung up the house phone. He called Joe a second time, telling him to be prepared to fly to London first thing in the morning. A few hours later his attorney emailed him the final agreement to go over. Leo went over all of the paperwork, the one that nullified the prenuptial and the new agreement replacing that. The documents would be drawn and ready first thing tomorrow morning, and Joe would deliver them to London for Caryn's signature. The money would hit her account the moment the documents were signed. That's how much clout Leonardo Vitale had. He would never have to see her again. Between the cash and the property he gave her, this endeavor had cost him over a billion dollars. Money well spent to get Caryn Richards out of his life.

It was after ten by the time Leo finished. As he walked past Rose's room, he could see a rectangle of light spilling out from under her door. He tapped lightly on the solid wood door.

"Come in," she said. Rose looked beautiful, sitting up against the pillows in his bed. He would love to take her in his arms and make love to her throughout the night the way they used to. Her luscious blond hair curled over her shoulders as she sat holding a book. Her skin looked translucent, and he was happy to see she'd gained some weight. The Sicilian sun had done wonders for her. The dark circles under her eyes and her pasty complexion were gone.

She belongs in this room in my bed always. Rose brushed her blond tresses back over her shoulder. Her pink satin nightgown clung to her breasts. A light comforter covered her legs. She put her book on the nightstand before she gazed at him. "I heard your helicopter earlier. I thought you'd left."

I never want to leave you. "No, I'm not going anywhere. I didn't want to bother you, but I saw your light on. I want you to know it's over between Caryn and me. I told her I'm not going to marry her."

Rose gasped before one delicate brow arched at him. "How did that go?"

He smiled, left out the money part, and said, "Pretty good. She's on her way back to London. No tears, no scene."

"Really? From the little I know of her, that seems so out of character. Well, I'm glad if it's what you want and not because of Isabella… or me."

I want both you and my daughter in my life. "No, you just made me realize what an awful mistake I was about to make."

"Then I'm happy for you… Can I ask you a favor?"

He came to the side of the bed. "Yes, anything."

"Tomorrow, I have a doctor appointment. Would you… come with me?"

"Yes, of course. It's late. You need your rest." He brushed a kiss on her temple and another on her cheek. Her scent filled the air around her, and a memory of Rose applying perfume to her freshly bathed body sent a jolt of blood into his groin… His voice was a husky whisper, "You found the bottle of perfume, the same as you used to wear."

"Yes, you remembered how much I liked the fragrance. You said it was the closest to what Sicily smelled like. I giggled at the time and thought how can a fragrance remind anyone of a place? Silly me, then when I came here and sat on the patio in the morning sun, I understood. I'm happy that you bought me the perfume." She sighed, and he fought to keep his hands at his side and not touch her, drag her into his arms, devour her sensuous lips.

"Good night," he whispered.

"Night… Leo, before you go, I want to thank you for all you've done for me. I'm so happy you can spend time with Isabella and bond with her. Thank you so much."

"No thanks necessary. You get strong and healthy. Tomorrow morning, before I escort you to your doctor appointment, I'd like to join you and Isabella for breakfast."

He watched as her eyes filled with happiness; her smile brightened the room. "Oh, I would love that, and I know Isabella would be so happy."

He couldn't help himself. He brushed her lips with a kiss. "A domani."

"Yes, Leo, until tomorrow."

ROSE ASKED Signora Santa Maria if she could have breakfast set up on the patio. The Sicilian morning sun wasn't very strong and perfect for them to sit at the outdoor table and enjoy the magnificent view of the Ionian

Sea while they ate. "Signore Vitale will join us this morning."

Rose learned early on that the staff was thrilled to help her. As they said, the American who spoke fluent Italian and her little girl had won their hearts.

This morning, Leonardo's chef prepared homemade yogurt with fresh berries and a drizzle of honey, with a pot of the rich Italian espresso she loved. For Isabella, the chef made pancakes in fun shapes.

"Good morning. How are you?" Leonardo, dressed in one of his custom-made suits, white shirt, and a silk tie, said as he walked out onto the patio. The puppy ran over, wagged its tail at Leonardo, and then went to sit next to her bowl by Isabella's chair.

"Papa, you here," Isabella said.

"Good morning," Rose said. "I asked Signora Santa Maria to set a plate for you, and she brought your favorite. Strong coffee and a jam-filled croissant."

Leonardo kissed Isabella on her cheek. "I see you're dressed as Belle today. Are you going to watch *Beauty and the Beast?*" Isabella shook her head, and her curls bounced. Leonardo moved to take his seat at the rectangular table. Izzy ate her pancakes, and Rose savored every drop of the homemade yogurt. Once breakfast was over, Nanny B came to take Izzy and the dog to Izzy's room.

"You behave. Papa is driving me to my appointment." She bent down to kiss Isabella and scratched the puppy behind its ear.

"Izzy be good."

Rose grabbed her purse from the end table, and then she and Leonardo walked out of the villa and around the stone path to the garage.

"Would you like me to come in to the doctor with you?" Leonardo said as they entered the garage.

"Oh, yes, would you? I would like that very much. My Italian is good, but I'm a little worried about the news."

He stopped mid-stride, and his head snapped in her direction. "What's wrong? At your last checkup, you said everything was on track, promising. All the broken bones are knitting nicely. No more concussion." He pushed a lock of his black hair back over his brow, and his blue gaze bore into her.

"My arm is… I'm not sure. My ribs are fine, the leg is great, but my arm cramps up. And the pain when that happens is terrible… and my fingers feel cold all of the time."

His chiseled features filled with concern as his black brows drew together. "Let's be sure to tell the doctor about that." He held her elbow and started walking again.

She rolled her eyes and didn't want to be treated like a child, but it felt good the way Leo helped her to get around. They walked in the underground garage, past a line of ultra-expensive cars.

"I don't know about your Lamborghini. I think it's too low to the ground for me to get in and out of."

"I can lift you and carry you, but I think you'll be more comfortable in the Mercedes."

"I'm not a child to be carried, Leo," she said firmly.

His deep voice held a huskiness as he said, "I know… Indulge me."

They stopped in front of his red Mercedes sedan. Leo opened the door for her. She managed to slide into the front seat with no help. He closed the door, and she fastened her seatbelt while Leonardo walked around to the driver's side.

The winding road to the business center of Taormina was breathtaking. She could see the picture-perfect landscape and the way the ancient Greco Roman Theater in the distance was situated, taking in the Bay of Naxos and Mount Etna. Today, plumes of smoke billowed into the sky from one of the most active volcanoes in the world. It was such an exciting place that she wanted to explore once she was steadier on her feet.

Once an archaeologist, always an archaeologist. She'd used the laptop Leonardo gave her to research the marvelous treasure. Built by the Greeks and then added to by the Romans, at present, it was used for concerts.

"Has your nurse told the doctor what's been going on with your arm?" Leo asked as he maneuvered a sharp turn.

"Yes, and that's why I have this appointment today."

"Good. I'm sure you want to correct this right away," he said in a tender tone.

She loved the way he cared for her. From the moment she woke up in the hospital and looked into his deep blue eyes, Leonardo promised to take care of her and Isabella. Gradually, as her strength and health improved, she would get more of her independence back. For now, leaning on him for support felt so good and right. From the minute they met until she left him, they were exclusive. He'd told her he was supposed to be in Rome, but he could work from anywhere as long as she was with him. She missed him and the time they'd shared. She would tread lightly, not wanting to put her heart on the line.

"I spoke to my grandmother this morning before I met you for breakfast. I told her about you and Isabella. She wants to meet you."

Her stomach clenched. "Does she hate me?"

Leonardo's blue gaze shifted in her direction. "How can anyone hate you? It thrilled my grandmother that she has a great granddaughter. She can't wait to meet you both. Nonna wanted to come over today, but with your doctor appointment and not knowing how that would go… I thought maybe we can ask her over for pranso, tomorrow. How do you feel about that?"

"Yes, I think we can all sit in the dining room… if you like. Nanny B can find the prettiest dress Isabella has and…" She took in a deep breath. "I hope… does she know you've broken off your engagement with Caryn?"

"Yes, on the phone this morning." He grinned at her. "Now, don't be nervous. She likes you already."

Rose sat back in the seat and lifted her brows. "How? She's never met me."

"Ahh, but you gave her something she never thought to have… a great-granddaughter. I know you'll like Nonna."

After the doctor's appointment, Rose asked Leonardo if she could see some of Taormina. Leonardo drove down to the beach. They parked, and he showed her the small island called Isola Bella, meaning beautiful island. "Once you're better, we can go there. At low tide, there's a strip of sand that we can walk across."

"Leo, it's early enough to ask you grandmother to come over today instead of waiting until tomorrow. I'm sure your chef can make enough food for one more person."

"If you're sure," he said as he lifted his cell phone from the console where he'd put it. He spoke into the phone, and then it connected to the car speakers. "Nonna, would you like to come to *pranso* today?"

Rose heard the excitement in the older woman's voice as she said yes. Then he hung up and turned to Rose. "Shall we go home?"

"Yes. *Si, andiamo a casa.*"

Leonardo's grandmother Lidia Vitale was a pleasant, petite woman with greying hair and the exact shade of blue eyes like Leonardo and Isabella. Her pink Chanel suit was trimmed in black. She wore black Chanel shoes with a low heel and carried a matching purse.

Lidia Vitale spoke in thickly accented English until Rose greeted her in Italian.

She pressed her hands to her cheeks. "Oh, my heart can't take any more; not only a beautiful great-granddaughter, but her mother speaks Italian as a native."

They entered the formal dining room. Sliding glass doors led out to a stone patio. Past the patio to one side was the pool and beyond that, the sea glinted like diamonds across its surface. In the dining room, the housekeeper had set the table with a starched white linen tablecloth, the edge hand crocheted in an intricate pattern. The linen napkin edges were crocheted in the same design. Isabella's booster seat was placed next to her.

"Enough drama. Nonna, come sit down before the food gets cold," Leonardo said as he shook his head. Then he grinned as he helped Isabella into her seat. "Nonna, sit here opposite Rose and Izzy." When Leonardo sat at the head of the table, the housekeeper began serving the first course. Rose felt joy bubbling in her at the way Leonardo's grandmother embraced Isabella and accepted her without question.

"You know, when Leonardo brought me to London to meet Caryn, it took all of my willpower not to say something negative. My English is not great, and she spoke no Italian, but we both spoke French, so at least we could converse. Leonardo took us to the theater, shopping, and dinner at some of the most exclusive restaurants. It all seemed so superficial and not what my grandson needed. But I said nothing. After all, I nagged and nagged him to find someone and get married, start a family. I don't know. My foolish old heart. My son, Leonardo's father, was terrible to Bella, Leo's mother. She came to me crying on more than one occasion, and I tried to talk to my son, but he was already too far gone in his world of women and drugs."

"Nonna, we don't want to drag up the past."

"I'm sorry, Rose; excuse an old lady."

"Mrs. Vitale, please, I don't mind, and you are not old. I hope Izzy and I will get to see more of you."

"Rose, if I'm not too presumptuous, I would like you to call me Nonna."

"I would be honored."

Once lunch ended, they went into the living room. Lady was allowed to come play with the squeaky toy that Leo's grandmother brought for her, and Izzy played with the doll that she got. She said to Isabella in her broken English, "I gonna teeche you Italian."

Isabella looked at her. "Like Mamma an Papa?"

"Si, yes, just like Mama and Papa." She turned to Rose. "I hope one day soon, when you are feeling stronger, you and Isabella and the puppy can come visit me. I'm sure Leonardo told you that my home isn't too far from here."

"I would love that. Thank you."

Before she went home, his grandmother said, "After all of my complaining and nagging you, I didn't know how I could ask you not to marry Caryn. I'm happy that you broke your engagement. Rose is so much better for you, and you've already made a daughter together."

"Nonna!"

"What? I was young once."

She smiled at Rose. "Come visit me soon."

HIS GRANDMOTHER HAD GONE HOME, and Izzy was with her nanny. The sun had set, and the first stars of the evening twinkled above. Leonardo and Rose went back into the house. He followed her to the sitting room. Rose switched on the lamps beside the sofa. The house was quiet, and he had to talk with her.

"Rose, I've stayed close to home so that Isabella and I

could really bond, but I have delayed some critical meetings long enough."

"Leo, please go. Take care of your business. We're fine here. Now we even have your grandmother to visit. I'm going to contact the director of the Pompeii dig and some of my acquaintances. Remember my friend Joan?"

"Yes, Davenport."

"She's in Calabria, and I want to visit her before Izzy and I go home. Really, Leo, you go. I know you're in the process of a big renovation of your hotel in Barcelona."

"Yes. I'll video chat as much as I can."

One day he found himself in Barcelona, sitting alone in a tapas bar, wishing Rose were with him. He missed her and Isabella so much that his heart ached. He finished his meeting and had Joe arrange for an immediate departure for home. On the flight back to Sicily, Leonardo spoke with Joe, "I want to stay closer to home and not travel so much. It's been a long time coming, and I feel you deserve this promotion. I've made a new position and included a hefty pay raise. You will make decisions in my absence without having to contact me."

"Mr. Vitale, I'm honored that you trust me. Thank you."

"I want to promote Lena as well. You can choose what position to give her, and you can interview for an assistant." Leo was happy to stay near the villa and not go on long business trips. He, Rose, and Izzy fell into a routine. Each day, they had breakfast together. Then he'd go to his study and work, have a video conference with Joe, or sit in on a meeting remotely. Then after pranzo during riposo, Izzy would nap, and he and Rose would sit on the patio or take a walk. Sometimes, they'd go for a drive.

One night after Isabella ate dinner, she asked, "Mama, Papa read Izzy story." Leonardo carried Isabella to her bedroom. Her nanny had turned down the pink satin comforter, and he and Rose both put her to bed.

After Isabella fell asleep, they walked out of her room and onto the terrace. They reclined on a double chaise lounge, overlooking the sea, having a martini before their dinner. She wore a mid-length silk sheath dress with a scoop neck.

"Leo, I'm happy that Isabella bonded with you so easily. The day they discharged me from the hospital, when I saw you holding her hand and walking out of your hotel in Texas, that's when I knew you'd be a wonderful and caring father."

Leo nodded before he said, "When I picked up Izzy from her temporary foster care family, I saw how nervous she was, and so was I. I worried because there had been so many changes for our little girl. She was quiet and held her doll to her, but when she came into my suite, and I took her into her bedroom, it affronted her when she saw the crib. Holding her doll, she looked up at me and said, 'Mamma say Izzy big girl sleep in bed. So, there we were in a three-bedroom suite, and all the beds were king size. I called down for a twin bed to be sent up. I got her into the bed and then I was going to place pillows on the floor, but she wanted me to read a story to her and her doll. Once she fell asleep, I stayed up all night watching her to make sure she didn't roll out onto the floor and hurt herself." He laughed. "In the morning, Frank came to the suite and found me sitting on her bed. I explained my predicament, and he asked why I didn't order rails? His sister uses them on her kids' beds. I laughed so hard. Guard rails, who knew."

Rose's musical laugh filled the air. "I never baby talked to her, and Isabella is very independent. She has a mind of her own. One day at the daycare, she watched as the older children drank out of cups without lids. She decided she was too big for a bottle or a sippy cup. That was the end of that. No more sippy cups. I thought I would have a difficult time weening her, but she did it all by herself. Same with the diapers. Need big girl panties. I tried to reason with her."

He laughed.

"You think it's funny? Reasoning with a two-year-old, yes, it is pretty funny. But no, she wouldn't let me put on the diaper. She made herself stiff as a board and said, 'No, no, me big girl.' I explained how she would have to let me know before she wet herself. She learned pretty quickly. I think she had only one accident that first night." Rose chuckled and took a sip of her martini. "I was fortunate that the university provided day care for students and faculty. I would visit her during my breaks and have lunch with her. Then, after class, we would walk home." She shuddered. "I'm grateful that I hired a sitter to watch her for my evening classes. I can't think if she were with me… that night."

Leo stood and walked around the double chaise lounge to kneel by her. "Don't do this, Rose. Don't make yourself upset. All is working out, and I'm meeting my daughter. You are here now, safe." He stood and took her hand. "Come, let's enjoy this quiet dinner, just the two of us. No talk of anything else. Remember how our favorite times were spent in each other's arms, lounging on the sofa, nibbling cheese, bread, and olives out of the same plate."

"I would be exhausted and sweaty from the dig, and you would have the tub filled for a relaxing bath and a quiet dinner set up for us."

"I loved our time together."

"Me too, Leo, me too."

At the table before they sat, he leaned into her and took her lips. She sighed and kissed him back. "My chef made this especially for you. He said that you liked the panelle he'd made. Street food is delicious — so he made you arancini, rice balls just for you. There is a history to these and as an archaeologist, you would appreciate it."

"Leo, he's gone out of his way to take care of me. All of your staff have been wonderful to me and Isabella. Thank you."

"No thanks necessary. You're easy to please, and they love Izzy. I know they are so thrilled you speak Italian with them."

"I think, along with your grandmother, they're teaching Isabella a word or two."

Rose sipped her wine before she took a bite of the meat filled rice balls his chef had made for them. Once the plates were removed, he meshed his fingers with her smaller ones, and they went to stand at the edge of the balcony, enjoying the beautiful Sicilian night. A slight breeze sent wisps of her hair to lightly brush his cheek. Blood rushed into his groin, and his erection pressed against his zipper. *What am I, a teenager?*

Leo was relieved that he and Caryn came to an understanding so that he was free to pursue Rose. He missed her terribly and now that she was stronger; he wanted to take her to bed and love her through the night. "Rose, I need you." He lowered his head and took her soft, sensuous lips with his.

She reached up, sliding her hands along his arms until they rested on his shoulders as she leaned into his body. "Leo," she breathed against his mouth.

He tugged her softness into his body. His hands gliding over the silk of her dress, over the roundness of her hips, slipping his hands to her buttocks as he pressed her body against him. The moonlight silvered her face as Rose gazed up at him. She brushed his lips with her finger. Leo watched the flame of desire ignite deep in the depths of her green eyes. "Yes, Leo, I've missed you so much."

"Say no now, and I will go to my room."

She leaned her lethal body into his. "I thought this was

your suite, and I've been sleeping in your bed. Don't go... Leo," she said in a throaty whisper.

His mouth swooped down on her inviting lips. Rose stepped into his embrace. She trembled in his arms and opened her mouth for him. He deepened the kiss, his tongue sliding into her mouth. She moaned as her smaller one tangled with his before she sucked his tongue. *Ahh, Rose, Rose.* Leo lifted her into his arms and carried her into the sitting room. They sat on the sofa. He held her in his arms, kissing her lips, her neck. His hand skimmed her body, and then he found her breast, massaging it through the silk fabric of her dress. Rose held his head and tugged him to her. She parted her lips to press on his, and his world exploded with her tender touch. He moved his mouth over hers, devouring the softness, and his tongue explored the recesses of her mouth, re-acquainting himself with this woman who touched his soul. Soft kisses, hard kisses, Leo held her, caressing her breast, and Rose clung to him as he devoured her mouth. He needed to go slow, but his body demanded he take her this minute. He kissed her neck, reaching his lips to the scoop of her silk dress.

Rose moaned and held him closer to her. "Leo, I need you." Her words filled him to bursting with desire. His Rose needed him as much as he needed her.

He slid her zipper down the curve of her back. Brushing the delicate fabric of her dress off her shoulders, Rose stood and shimmied her dress down her body. It silently pooled at her feet. She looked thinner than he remembered, but her body was as lethal as ever, with a faint stretch mark from childbirth and rounder hips. Her breasts in the sheer bra were as enticing as always. Her erect nipples pointed against the cups.

"Leo, stop staring."

"Your beauty, my precious Rose, has rendered me speechless and reminded me of how much I need you."

She reached her hands up and unhooked her bra. His groin throbbed as he watched them bounce free. He took over, holding her to him. Kissing her lips, caressing her breasts, then he moved his mouth lower along the column of her neck. The excited beat of her pulse tapped against his lips. He savored the moment before he dragged his mouth along to the rise of her breasts, reaching for a pointed nipple he couldn't help but engulf it into his mouth. Rose moaned, and her fingers brushed his hair before she cupped his head to hold him closer.

He licked her nipple. "Oh, Leo, yes."

His hand slid along her smooth skin, over her belly. She kissed his neck, and unbuttoning his shirt, she stroked his shoulders, sliding his shirt over his biceps. He moved to her other breast, doing the same kissing, sucking the nipple into his mouth. His hand slid lower along her abdomen, past the elastic band of her panties.

Rose moved closer and raised herself on her toes. Leo mentally smiled at how eager his love was for him. He slid his finger along her slit. She moaned his name. He slipped his middle finger in her, feeling how wet she was for him.

"Ahh, Rose, so nice." He lifted her into his arms and carried her to the bedroom. Her fingers dug into his hair. The bedside lamp cast the room in shadows, lighting only the bed in a soft yellow glow. He lay her in the center of the cotton sheets. He ripped his shirt off and unzipped his pants. Stepping out of them, he came to lie next to Rose.

She looked like a goddess; her blond hair spread out in ripples over the pillow. Her kiss-swollen lips, her breasts—*God, she is beautiful* — the pink nipples extended, the areolas puckered and wet from his mouth. He had to taste her. He craved her flavor all these years. No other woman came close to Rose. Leo kissed her belly and slowly slid her panties off her hips. His lips followed as her delicate skin was revealed to his mouth. He brushed the scrap of satin and lace down to her thighs, then to her knees.

"Oh Rose, your beauty–"

"Leo, I need you."

He kissed her abdomen with open-mouth kisses, dragging his lips along her satin-smooth flesh, needing to drink her skin in. She ran her fingers through his hair, her nails teasing his scalp.

"Just one dip of my tongue in your sweet sex."

"Yes, Leo, yes."

He snaked his tongue out and licked up her slit. He slipped his tongue into her center. She tasted better than he could possibly remember, without going insane. Her fingers pressed into his head. Leo needed no more invitation than that. His sweet Rose needed this as much as he wanted it. He slipped her panties off her legs and dropped them to the floor. "Let me know if anything hurts."

"I will. Right now, everything feels really good."

He smiled at that before his fingers parted the tuft of blond hair, and he buried his tongue in her, licking and tracing her inner lips before sucking her glistening folds. She arched her back, and he worried about her ribs, so he lifted her legs over his shoulders, being very gentle of her injured leg.

"I love your care of me, Leo, but I'm not made of glass." She cupped his head and pressed him to her.

He paid her back by sucking her clit into his mouth.

"Ohhh yesss." He didn't give her time to say more as he licked and kissed her, taking his time loving her clit, before he thrust his tongue deep into her.

Rose's abdominal muscles tightened at the same time her inner thighs quivered. "Leo," she panted before her shallow breath increased with her excitement. He felt the first tiny pulse of her vagina on his tongue.

"Ahh, ahh, yes." Her throaty voice floated around him. He slipped his hands under her buttocks and lifted her more firmly to his mouth.

Her hands slipped to grip the sheets, and she dug her heels into his shoulders, moving her hips in tiny erotic circles. Leonardo used his thumbs to keep her open as he buried his tongue into her hot pussy. Savoring the flavor of his Rose before licking up to her clit.

"God, yes, Leo, suck it."

He did.

Her breath hissed out of her as her core muscles contracted. She reached her hands into his hair, her fingers tugging him to her. "Oh, oh Dio mio, Leo," she moaned.

He tasted the ripples of her climax against his mouth.

She lay back panting, and her feet fell from his shoulders. She was his wild Rose, and he had to have her back in his life. He loved her. He'd never stopped loving her.

"Ahh Rose. I'll go slow."

"I don't know if I want you to go slow. I want you deep in me now… But Leo, I'm not on any birth control."

He groaned before he placed a kiss on her lips. "I don't trust myself to pull out. I'll be right back." He slipped his pants back on. "Don't move."

She smiled up at him. "I won't but hurry."

He slipped out of the bedroom and went down the hall to get his condoms.

He grabbed a handful and when he returned, he threw them on to the nightstand.

Rose held her arms out to him, and he lay down and pulled her on top of him. "I'm not fragile, and you don't have to treat me with kid gloves."

"I'll be the judge of that."

She giggled and ran her hands down his chest. Reaching for his erection, she wiggled her brows at him and said, "We'll see." Her hand moved on his excited flesh, stroking him. "I like… when you…" She looked into his eyes, and he saw the uncertainty. Her words tugged at his heart. "Leo, after I went home… there has only been you."

"Shh, my sweet wild Rose. He flipped her over, and she giggled, running her hands over his shoulders and down his arms. "Mmm, I can't wait."

He gazed into her unique eyes, with the brown center and their emerald-green outer ring.

He slipped his hand down her body, his fingers kneading her breasts, kissing her as he sucked a nipple into his mouth. She arched her back, offering more to him. He hungered for her, for this woman who he'd never forgotten. How could he think that he could have married someone else? He cleared his mind of all thoughts but his precious Rose, and her scent drifted around him as he kissed her skin, between the valley of her breasts, to the pouting nipple that needed his attention. She moved under him, spreading her legs as her hands drove him crazy. She slid her hands along his back; her nails teased and scraped his skin. He groaned. *Slow, slow, slow*, he chanted to himself.

She must have realized his plan because she smiled up into his eyes just as her fingers wrapped around his already massive erection. "Rose," he groaned.

"I need you in me now.… See how ready I am for you."

His finger slid into her moist body. He held her eyes while he swirled his middle finger in her. "Yes, I can feel your desire," he said. Leo grabbed one of the condoms and ripped the packet open with his teeth. He rolled onto his back. Rose knelt on the mattress with a bewitching smile as she watched him. His hand trembled, and he was amazed at the depth of his need as he rolled the condom on. He felt a thrill of desire race through his body.

Rose didn't waste a second. She tugged him to lie over her. "Please, I need you now." She moved her hips.

He held her to him and tried for gentle. She spread her legs and, taking him in her hand, guided Leo to her entrance. "Hurry please, Leo."

He held his control as he gradually slipped into her heat. The heat and tightness of her body was too much, he had to move. He thrust into her, pulling out and thrusting to the hilt again and again. Rose followed, catching the rhythm and moving to take more of him into her body. It was over too quickly as she moaned and writhed against him. He didn't know if he could wait any longer, his control slipping. Then she arched her back, and her breasts rubbed on his chest. Her arms tightened around his neck at the same time as her legs wrapped around his hips. Locking her ankles, she pressed her little heels into the middle of his back.

A delicious heat built and spread from his back along to his groin. He gritted his teeth, desperate for control, holding back his own rising pleasure, as moisture popped on his brow.

"Oh Leo, yes, yes. You feel so good." Rose pulsed around him. Each glorious contraction drew him closer to release. He shouted as pleasure erupted through his body, and a mind-blowing orgasm brought him release. Leonardo held his weight off her passion-filled body. Their breaths heavy, he looked at her. The fringe of her lashes covered her eyes, and a smile spread across her lips. "Mmm, Leo." She opened her eyes. "It's not a dream."

"No, this is very real and, oh, so good. To have you back in my arms and in my bed. I love you."

She kissed him. "I love you too."

Just before dawn, she said, "Isabella will be up soon, and I don't think it will be good for her to see us in bed… The staff, my nurse, and the nanny will be up and moving around soon."

"Yes, I'll go back to the other room." He couldn't call it his bedroom any longer. We would have to let Izzy adjust to this. He smoothed her thick, long hair back from her face, tucking a curl behind her ear as he kissed her lips.

He kissed her again before he slipped on his pants and gathered the remainder of his clothes. He scooped up her clothes and laid them on the bedside chair. He opened the nightstand drawer and swiped the rest of the condoms into it. He shrugged and tipped his head to one side. "We'll need these for later while Izzy naps and tonight."

At the sparkle in her eyes, he fought the urge to climb back into bed with her. "Yes. In the meantime, will you have breakfast with us?"

"Yes, my wild Rose. I'll come back at breakfast. Right now, you go to sleep."

LEONARDO WENT BACK to his room. It was small and cramped compared to the master bedroom. He showered and dressed, going over every minute of last night. Holding Rose in his arms erased all the feeling of loss he suffered when she left him. He'd buried it so deep down in his mind that he hadn't realized how much she'd hurt him. He was glad she was back, but this time, not willing to take a chance with his heart again, things would be different. When he realized that she'd left him, he threw himself headfirst into work. Ten months had gone by before he lifted himself up from that dark place.

He wanted to be a father to Isabella and a lover to Rose. He and Rose spent their days together, eating all their meals as a family. He cringed each time he thought of the mistake he'd almost made with Caryn.

He enjoyed how they would both read to Izzy, and once she fell asleep, he and Rose would walk out to the terrace to have a late dinner. Tonight was no different. His housekeeper set an intimate table for them. The evening air was warm, and the candle flames danced in the slight breeze. Late June in Sicily was just as delightful as May. The night was calm, with no sound. Taking the chilled champagne from the bucket, he popped the cork. "Three weeks without pain medication. I think it calls for a celebration."

"Yes, and my arm is one hundred percent better. The pinched nerve in my neck caused all that added trouble, but the massages and therapy have definitely helped. I know how lucky I was."

"Yes, you were very lucky." He cringed every time he thought of how different it could have gone, how she may have died, and he would never have met his daughter.

"It is a significant milestone for me. I'm able to be without a nurse and therapist. Ms. Carrington was wonderful, and I'm grateful that you gave her a six-month wage salary bonus. That was very generous of you, Leo. I hope our references help her get another position. She was professional and very compassionate."

"Yes, I called the agency and spoke directly with her supervisor, telling them how great she was."

"I'll make plans for Isabella and me to head back to Texas."

"What? It is much too soon for that. We have to settle our differences."

She smiled at him and shook her head. "We don't have any differences, Leo. Back in Texas, I have a life. I actually like teaching at the community college. I wasn't sure at first and thought I settled for that position because I was pregnant, but no, I really enjoy my career. Maybe one day I'll find the time to work toward my PhD." She shrugged a shoulder. "If that doesn't happen, it will be okay… On the matter of our differences, as you say, what's the real reason you've broken your engagement to Caryn? It can't be because she yelled at the dog and made Izzy cry."

"No, there's more to it… When I returned from Morocco and found you and Isabella exercising on your yoga mats in the sunroom, I knew I wanted to be a part of that. I wanted—Why didn't you let me know about Isabella?"

Rose's blond hair curled over one shoulder. She gazed up. "We've been through that. I followed you in the papers and magazines. Your engagement was front page news—"

He shrugged. "That was a year ago. What about the time before, while you were pregnant or when Isabella was born?" *She's so cool the way she's ignoring me.*

"When I read about your engagement, it didn't take me long to figure out that it was only me you didn't want a marriage with."

"That's not true," he shouted before he clenched his teeth. She was the only one who could make me lose my temper. Regaining his composure, he said, "I wanted to tell you that night. I never wanted to marry or have children—"

"See, you're saying those exact words again." Rose snapped. "Your rejection was hurtful then and now."

"I'm sorry, but you did not let me finish what I wanted to say that night. You excused yourself to the restroom. Do you know how long I sat there waiting for you to return? I asked the restaurant manager to send someone in to look for you, to make certain you weren't hurt or sick. 'No, Miss Steele is not in the restroom.' I drove down to your hotel and was told you'd checked out. Your belongings would be forwarded to you once you gave them an address. My hotel and I couldn't get any information. I was furious with you, the way you left me."

"Well, how do you think I felt? My hormones were on overdrive, and I'd prepared to tell you I was pregnant. Then you say that you never want to marry."

"This is your fault. Had you let me finish what I was going to say then, perhaps we wouldn't be in this situation at present."

"Oh, so you're laying the blame for this on me as if it's my fault?"

He wouldn't be gallant. "Yes, it is… I was going to propose to you. I had a ring and all. I wanted to tell you that although I feared turning into my father, I wanted you in my life. You made me a better person, and I would never cheat on you or hurt you in any way at all… I love you."

Her eyes downcast, she murmured, "I don't know what happened, but I didn't want to be hurt by the only man I've ever loved." She gazed into his eyes. "Leonardo—"

"Shh… Do you hear that?"

Her perfect brows came together. "Music?"

"More than music, it is our song."

"Oh, yes." Her long lashes drifted down over her eyes, the beginning of a smile on her lips, and she swayed in her seat to the gentle strings of the song.

"Will you dance with me?" He extended his hand.

She gazed up into his eyes. Rose put her hand in his and stood. She stepped into the circle of his arms. He held her in a tender embrace. She looked so much better, no longer fragile. His chef had done wonders with her diet. "Rose, you're beautiful."

She leaned against him, and he placed a soft kiss on her brow, brushing his lips along her temple to her soft cheek. She turned her face and lifted onto her toes.

All the years they'd missed seeped into his soul. He held

her in his embrace and dipped his head. His lips brushed her sweet lips. Rose sighed, and he was lost. Slanting his mouth against hers, he opened her mouth, and her little tongue met his, swirling and twining as he held her and swayed to the gentle sound of the music. Holding her, kissing her, loving her, needing Rose as no other. She was here, and he would do anything in his power to keep her here with him. The years without her were empty, and he didn't want that again.

He moved to the music, and she followed, swaying against him. She looped her silky-smooth arms around his neck. Her fingers made sensuous circles at the nape of his neck. She twined one finger into his hair. Holding her tiny waist, the silk fabric of her dress bunched in his hands, he tugged her into him.

"Mmm, Leonardo, I've missed you so much."

"Rose, Bellissima, Rose."

They swayed to the gentle strings of the music. Holding her hips to his, wanting her to know how much he needed her.

She melted in his arms.

He carried her into his bedroom and stood her in front of the mirror. Wrapping his arms around her, he caught her gaze in the reflection. He pressed a kiss to her ear before he whispered, "I need you."

Rose lifted her arm to stroke his hair. She shifted her neck, and his lips descended on the soft flesh, kissing her. He slid his hand down her body, reaching the hem of her dress. He slipped his hand under the fabric and searched out her panties. He found her center warm and ready for him.

Rose turned in Leonardo's arms. "Keep doing that, and I'll come right here."

His smile melted her as his finger found her again. "Is that so bad?" he said, sliding his thumb over her clit.

"No, it's wonderful. Ahh… so nice." Rose lifted her dress over her head and dropped it to the floor. Leonardo knelt and tugged her to him. She hooked her thumbs in the elastic of her panties and shimmied them down her legs. "Leo, I can't wait—"

His big, powerful hands held her to him as he sank his tongue into her wet heat. Rose cried out and came in a gush of pleasure undulating against him.

She smiled at the rasp of his zipper. "Yes, Leo, here." He stood and lifted her to him. She looped her arms around his neck as he settled her on his throbbing erection. "Is this good? Your leg?"

"Yes, Leo, so very good." He lifted and lowered her on his erection until she came again. Then he carried her to the bed, grabbed a condom, and started all over again.

CHAPTER 6

In the morning, Rose and Isabella sat to breakfast when Leonardo walked in to join them. Freshly showered and shaved, his soapy clean scent drove her crazy. An image of them in bed last night flashed before her eyes. His lean, naked body hovered above hers as he thrust into her over and over again. Her hands slid over his hard, rippling muscles, and then he muffled her screams of pleasure with his lips.

"Good morning." He brushed a kiss on her cheek, and his cologne teased her senses.

"Morning," she murmured.

He kissed Isabella.

"Izzy, don't play with your food."

"Want cookie."

"I think there are pancakes on the tray. Shall I get you one?" Leonardo asked.

"Yes, peeez."

She chuckled. "There are pancakes, because Papa has a sweet tooth."

"Like Izzy, Mama."

"Yes, exactly like you."

"Why don't you and I go to Capri? I bought a villa there last year and turned it into an intimate hotel."

She switched to Italian as she said, "Little ears hear everything, Leo. I don't want to leave her."

"She'll be fine with Nanny B. Let's go to Capri for a long weekend. I think Izzy will be okay with her nanny. It's only Capri, not the other side of the world."

"I know, but after… well, I can't be away from her." She couldn't bear to be apart from Izzy, and she wanted to spend time with Leo before they went back home to Texas.

Leonardo stretched his hand across the table and took her fingers, rubbing his thumb along her knuckles. Zings of electricity ran up her arm. She gazed at him, and he mouthed, "Ti ammo," before he continued in Italian, "We'll all go."

He never offered more than what they had. Lovemaking and always saying he loved her, but nothing more than that. "Okay, that sounds like fun."

That afternoon, they boarded Leo's helicopter for the ride to Capri. It was true she loved the island, and the archaeologist in her knew why Capri was so beautiful. The vegetation on the island was so grand, the lemons and fruits were larger than normal because the volcanic ash from Vesuvius, that buried the towns of Pompeii and Herculaneum traveled across the sea, covering the island as it spread.

Of course, he owned one of the best hotels in Capri, surrounded by luxury boutiques and nightclubs, including one he owned. This villa that he'd transformed into a smaller hotel was in the heart of Anacapri. The atmosphere here was relaxed and laid back with meandering trails through some of the most beautiful gardens in Italy. Leo gave Nanny B and Isabella their own suite, and he and Rose shared a very private suite on the top floor of the villa.

She tugged Leo by his belt to her. Leo lifted her in his arms and carried her into the bedroom. She needed him as never before. It was almost as if the three years had never happened, although she was pregnant for part of them.... He turned to switch on the lights, but instead of lights, the ceiling silently opened, and a round mirror the size of the bed appeared. The mirror would reflect whatever happened on the bed. The wall behind the round bed was covered with more mirrors. "Leo, oh my."

"This was the previous owner's master bedroom and definitely a room for lovemaking."

"Yes, it certainly is." He held her to him, unzipping her dress. "I have missed you." He brushed his lips along her neck.

Tingles of desire raced through her body. "We made love this morning," she teased him.

He nipped her shoulder. "Yes, that was too long ago."

She smiled, loving his hands on her and his playful kisses. "We had better not wait too long." Her dress slid down her body. His blue eyes sparked, and her nipples tightened at the way he looked at her in her lacy bra and thong. "I love you more than I thought possible."

He kissed her neck, running his tongue along the curve of her breasts, dipping into the cleavage.

"Oh, God, Leo." She held him to her.

"Rose, I want you so much. I thought to go slow and pay tribute to your body."

Leonardo unhooked her bra and brushed the satin straps down her arms. He stopped to kiss her arm, where it had been broken, and then he followed the bra. He held her breasts, and Rose held back the moan of sheer pleasure as he licked and sucked first one nipple and then the other. She was on fire and tried to unbutton his shirt. He brushed her hands away and kissed a line down her torso. Kneeling before her, he kissed her belly, her abdomen, then he lifted his gaze to her and slid her thong down her legs. A shiver of delight zapped through her body as his mouth brushed her mound. "I have to taste you," he said, and his tongue dipped into her, circling her clit, and she reached to hold his shoulders.

Leonardo stood and lifted her to sit on the edge of the round bed. The cool sheets sent a shiver up her heated body. Leo gently spread her knees as she reclined, resting on her elbows. He ran his hand along her stomach. He dipped his head and kissed her inner thigh, first one and then the other.

"Yes, Leo, yes." Her head tipped back, and she saw herself in the mirror above the bed. She'd forgotten about the mirror but looked at herself and Leo. Her pelvis flooded with hot desire. Rose lay against the red satin sheets, her thighs spread, and Leo's head between her legs. His black hair and the rippling muscles of his back were all she could see in the mirror. The sensation of his tongue licking and thrusting into her while she watched was the most erotic thing he'd ever done. She couldn't turn away from the mirror.

He slid his hands under her buttocks and lifted her to his mouth. She held back a moan when his thumbs spread her open, and her pelvis flooded. Leonardo thrust his wicked tongue so deep into her, he stroked her g-spot. Her torso bowed, and the sight of her breasts and excited nipples, wet from his mouth, added to her pleasure. "Ahh, ahh." Zaps of bliss vibrated into her core. "Oh, God." Her hand moved to her breast, and he pressed his tongue on her clit. "Leo." She moaned. He licked her clit. Her knees bent on his broad shoulders, Leo shifted his hands on her buttocks, lifting her firmly to his mouth as she pushed forward, sending his tongue deeper. He thrust and curled his tongue into her core.

"Leo… Leo." Her hands stroking his head, her fingers tangled in his thick, black hair.

He slid one hand from her buttock to guide her ankle and placed her foot on the edge of the mattress. She moved her other foot to the mattress, and Leo's tongue sank deeper into her. Again, he stroked her g-spot on his way to licking her clit.

"Leo, yes, oh God… suck… my clit. Ahh yes," she moaned at the first pulsing of her orgasm. Another pulse and another, Leo slid a finger into her and then another. She shuddered as waves of pure bliss filled her. Her pelvis curled, and her thighs squeezed, holding him to her.

She couldn't hold back the pleasure as he sucked her clit again. Waves and waves of pleasure contracted her vagina… He crooked his finger on her g-spot, and a second climax snuck up on her. Her heart pounded as she held him to her, and her legs were like jelly.

Leo took a condom from his pocket and threw it on the mattress before he stripped off his clothes. "Are you ready for more?"

"Yes, anything you want. I need your dick in me."

"I love it when you talk dirty. Show me what you want, wild Rose." He kissed her mouth, and she tasted herself.

Rose groaned and reached her hand between their bodies. She wrapped her fingers as far as she could around his massive erection. She gazed into his blue eyes, while her thumb ran along the velvety smooth head of his erection. "You feel so good, so big. I need you deep in me."

She held him at her entrance, then curled her pelvis, and lifted her hips. "Wait, Bellissima, a condom."

Her hand fell away from him. She groaned, "Okay, hurry."

Leo lifted her, and her legs slid on either side of him, with her knees on the mattress and he on his knees. Rose straddled him as he lifted and lowered her onto his erection. She held his shoulders as he pistoned into her. She felt another orgasm stroking him into her. "Yes, Rose, like that, yes." She leaned forward and muffled her scream in the crook of his powerful neck.

"Ahh, Rose," he groaned, lifting her.

"I love the feel of you deep in me," she murmured, sprinkling kisses on his neck and shoulders. She dragged her tongue along his pecs, tasting the salty dampness that covered his olive complexion.

She lifted her fingers to his cheeks and teased his lips with a kiss. He was hot and hard, the tendons in his powerful neck taut. Rose tightened her inner muscles, and Leonardo growled as he climaxed. She loved the feel of him and tightened her inner muscles, taking his long length into her. Leonardo held her, and she did it again, stroking him again as he shouted out in pleasure.

They lay in a puddle of sheer ecstasy. He stroked her hair from her face and kissed her lips. "Ti ammo, Rose."

"And I love you, Leonardo."

"I'll be right back, Amore. The condom slipped."

They fell asleep entwined in each other's arms. In the night, Rose rolled over onto Leo. He kissed her, found more protection, and then she straddled him. They made slow, sleepy love. In the morning, she awoke first, taking him into her mouth. His fingers burrowed into her hair. Sliding through her long hair, he cupped her head. "Am I dreaming? Oh, no, so much better than a dream."

They showered together and then went for a drive along the winding road down to the Grand Marina, where Leonardo had a boat waiting for them. He took the boat out, and they went around the island to the green grotto. It was much quieter, and there were no lines like there were by the famous blue grotto. "This is nice, Leo. We saw the blue grotto the last time we were on Capri, so this is definitely less crowded and hectic."

"Very secluded here, just you and me. I brought a picnic for us."

They lazed on the boat and drank wine while they ate wedges of cheese and hunks of crusty, fresh-baked bread. Leonardo lay on his side, and Rose memorized his broad chest, his thick neck, and his handsome face. "Wanna go below and—"

"Yes, always, yes."

"You don't even know what you're agreeing to."

"Oh yes, I do. You want my pussy, and I want your dick."

He laughed. "I love your enthusiasm." He jumped to his feet and tugged her up, then they went below deck.

ISABELLA THRIVED, playing with her puppy. Nanny B would take her down to the children's pool so she could play. Even the dog joined in the fun, learning how to swim. They talked about Isabella and although they shared a bed, they hid it from Isabella. Rose had a healthy sun-kissed glow to her fair skin. All signs of the induced coma and its groggy side effects were gone. Her bones healed, and she was taking longer and longer walks with Leo.

They were back from their idyllic vacation after two weeks. Rose's doctor had given her permission to drive, and Leonardo said she could use any car she wanted, but perhaps an automatic and not a manual transmission would be better.

One morning after breakfast, while Leo would be busy with video meetings and Nanny B had the day off, she took Isabella and Lady to drive down to his grandmother's house. It wasn't far, and this gave Rose back some of the independence she'd lost after her accident. They enjoyed spending time with her. Lidia Vitale was a wonderful person, and she seemed happy about their visit. They ate pranzo together, and then she and Nonna sat out in the beautiful garden, while Isabella and Lady napped in the shade. She had such a pleasant time with Leo's grandmother. Then, when Izzy awoke, they said goodbye and drove back to Leo's villa.

Leonardo was still locked in his study. Nanny B returned and took Isabella to watch a movie. Rose reclined in the sitting room, ready to read when Leonardo strolled in. "Did you and Izzy have a nice day with my grandmother?"

"Yes, we did. She cooked a fabulous lunch, and Izzy helped." Rose laughed. "She was covered in flour and tomato sauce. Luckily, I brought a change of clothes for her."

He sat on the sofa next to her. "It sounds like she had fun... I have to go to London. It can't be avoided. I have put this off longer than I should have. I promoted Joe, so I didn't need to travel as much, but there are some things that I as the owner of Vitale Hotels, have to do. I'll be away at least a week, in meetings most of the time. Otherwise, I'd say come with me, but it won't be much fun."

"I understand. Isabella and I will be eagerly waiting for your return. Then when you get back, we can all go to Calabria and visit my friend."

He frowned at her. "Where is Izzy?"

"She's with Nanny B. I'll go change for dinner." She went into the dressing room. Leo followed her and used his body to press her against the wall. She did not know what she'd done, but he was hard as granite against her back. His hand slipped around her waist and lower to the hem of her mini dress. He ran his big, warm hand up her leg and into the elastic at the front of her panties. "Spread them." His hot breath sent goosebumps up her body.

She did as he said, anticipating all the pleasure he would give her. "Oh, yes."

"How many?" he whispered

"Oh, Leo..." He nudged his dick against her back,

pressing her into the wall. He cupped her chin with his other hand, turned her head, and took her lips in a hungry, demanding kiss. His finger swirled deep in her before he traced her inner folds and used the slightest pressure on her clit. "How many?"

"Three… no four. I want four orgasms before you come." She bent her knees and moved her hips. He added a second finger, thrusting into her.

"Ah Rose, shall I make you beg as well before I give you release?"

"No, just make me come," she groaned.

"Let's see." His fingers slipped into her again, and she felt his smile before he nipped her lower lip. "You are so ready." He moved from her.

"Leo, no. Here against the wall. Just like this."

His smile melted her, and the spark in the depths of his blue eyes made her groan. She loved when he became all alpha male. They had the best mind-blowing sex then. Making love with Leo was always mind blowing, but when he prevented her from climaxing, and he'd start over again, well, it was great. She'd beg and scream, but he was a patient lover, and he'd wait until she whimpered in need.

"Okay, just like this, but this one won't count towards the four."

She pressed her forehead on the cool wall. He leaned into her, and then he used his big hands on her. One hand, with his fingers splay, slid over her belly, down her abdomen into her panties to rest on her mound, and the other brushed her breasts.

"Spread your legs," he whispered against her ear, then he ran his tongue along the rim before sucking her lobe into the heat of his mouth. She moaned and moved her feet further apart. "So nice, Rose." His hand warm against her breast, his fingers plucked her nipple. He surrounded her, his muscles flexing as he moved. She breathed in his scent, making her wild with need. He pressed his knee between her legs, pushing her into the wall. She stood on her toes, and his finger went deeper into her vagina. She pressed back on his thick, muscled thigh.

Leo whispered, "Raise your hands to the wall, palms flat above your head." She did, and a zing of excitement raced through her body.

"Yes, just like that." His husky whisper tightened her nipples.

She rotated her hips. "Oh, oh."

His fingers stilled, deep in her vagina.

"You said you wouldn't," she groaned.

"I lied," Leo said and turned her in his powerful arms. Holding her waist, he knelt.

"Are you okay?"

"Yes, just make me come."

"Let me know if—"

"Leo, I'm fine. My leg is strong, my arm is great, the ribs… hurry and get these clothes off me and make me come." She watched the smile spread across his lips.

He lifted her dress up, and she pulled it over her head, throwing it to the floor. Then she unhooked her bra. Leonardo pulled her hips to him before he slid her panties down her thighs to her knees. She pressed her back to the wall, and her fingers went into his thick, black hair. He pulled her to his mouth and spread her open for his tongue.

"God, I can't wait," she said, pressing herself to his mouth. His tongue snaked into her, and she held back the moan. He was so good at what he did, and she couldn't wait. He licked and sucked her until she came in a wave of undulating pleasure. Leo held her in his powerful embrace as her knees gave out, and she almost slid down the wall. He stood, lifting her out of the panties. She unbuttoned his shirt and when she reached to unzip his fly, he brushed her hands away.

"Remember… four times before it's my turn, so let's leave him right where he is in my pants." He lifted her into his arms and carried her to the bed.

"Leo, remember all the fun we had on chairs and standing in the middle of the room?"

"Oh yes, I remember so much. So, the chair it is. Kneel on the cushion and place your hands on the back. Bend over."

"Oh, God, yes, one of my favorites."

"I know, Amore." He unzipped his pants and pressed into her. She was so slick, and he inched into her until he was buried to the hilt, his fingers curling around her hips. She came twice in that position, then Leo carried her over to the bed. "Two more, and then I get to come."

THE NEXT DAY, Leo dressed in one of his custom-made suits. He sat with her and Isabella, having coffee and a roll. He laughed and joked with them. Isabella said she wanted to watch *Lady and the Tramp* today. After breakfast, he kissed her and ran his knuckle along her cheek. "I love you, Rose." He kissed Izzy, and he scratched Lady behind the ear. "We can video chat later."

She and Isabella sat at the breakfast table and in the distance, she heard his helicopter as he left for his business trip. Her heart tugged, missing him already.

"Papa come back soon?"

"Yes, darling, soon." She willed the seven days to whiz by.

CARYN STROLLED into the villa as if she owned the place. She was back. "What are you doing here? Leonardo is away on a business trip, and he won't be home for a few more days."

"I know he's in London. We've spent several wonderful days in bed together. He's a great lover, but I guess I don't have to tell you that. I came to see you, woman to woman."

She held herself together, refusing to let Caryn see how upset her words made her.

"We have nothing to talk about."

"Oh, but we do. You see, I'm here to make you an offer. I'm pregnant, and Leo––She flashed her engagement ring at Rose–– and I are going to elope tomorrow. It might be best if you aren't here when we return from our honeymoon. I'm prepared to give you one million dollars so that you can start over wherever you like—"

"I don't want your money," she sneered.

"Suit yourself, but I just need you to understand that you can't stay here. Leo said that you've fully recuperated. I can have your bags packed so you and Isabel can catch a flight back to wherever it is you live." She fluttered her fingers in the air.

Rose wasn't sure how to handle this. She and Leo spoke every day. Most times twice once so he could talk to Isabella and then at night to wish her good night. He'd say how he wished he were in bed with her and how he missed them both.

How could he do that? Be with Caryn and lie about wanting me. Was this what Leo meant? How he was like his father and unable to be with only one woman. The last time when she said she needed to go home, he didn't try to dissuade her or argue with her about it. *Maybe he's grown bored with me. I have to call him, talk to him before I do anything.*

"Leo came back, wanting me again. When I told him I was pregnant, and the only way I'd go back to him is if we would be married, he agreed. Now, I'm here to tell you that you will have to go. Today. Right now! I want to get the villa ready for us. When we get back from our honeymoon, I want no reminders that you were ever here."

Her body jolted, and her knees grew weak as a memory of those words hit her, almost knocking the breath out of her.

"My husband doesn't know about you, and I want no reminders of you and my past."

She was fifteen when she searched for her biological mother. Once Rose told her foster mother that she needed to see her biolog-ical mother, her foster mother had gone with her for support. Her mother opened the door and wouldn't allow Rose in. "I have a new family now."

"Can you at least tell me why you gave me away?"

She'd begun to close the door. "No, go now."

"Wait, please, what about my father? Can you tell me about him?"

"He's dead." She'd closed the door on Rose and her foster mother.

Now she stared at Caryn and swallowed past the lump in her throat, fighting the sting in her eyes. She couldn't talk, or the tears would just pour out of her. She collapsed onto the sofa. Bowing her head, she folded her trembling hands in her lap. A tear splashed onto the back of her hand, then another and another.

"I'll send the maid in to pack your and Isabel's things. I brought a dog carrier, and the mutt can stay in the cabin on the plane with you and Isabel. The taxi will be here in an hour, and your flight is at five p.m. this evening."

All that Rose could manage was to nod. She couldn't even look at Caryn. She won, and Leo the louse couldn't even tell her face to face. What did he expect her to cling to him and never let him go? That's what she wanted, but he wanted something else. Not her or his daughter. *He really is like his father. How will I explain to Izzy that we are leaving?* She went through the motions, not sure how.

Her biological mother's words, *I want no reminders* echoed in her brain over and over. The only happy memory of that day was when her foster mother hugged her and said, "Too bad. She will never know what she's missing and how special you are. I love you and am so happy that you came into my life. I couldn't ask for a better daughter." She'd kissed her and wiped her tears. Then they boarded the plane to head back home. At home, they'd told her foster father, and he'd had the same reaction, hugging her and telling her she was their daughter and how proud they were of her.

Rose took a deep, shaky breath, angry at herself for allowing Caryn to see her cry. She was stronger than that and focused on the next couple of hours and the days to follow.

Nanny B would fly back with them, but she couldn't afford to keep Isabella's nanny on her salary. Actually, the nanny made more than she did at the community college. Isabella would have to go back to daycare. The fall term had begun, and she'd have to wait until January and the spring semester to begin before she could teach again. How would she pay the rent on her one-bedroom apartment? Leo had paid the rent through the end of September, even though he wanted her to stay with him in Sicily. Men are so fickle, because now she was out, and Caryn was in. She knew better than to trust him, saying one thing and doing another. Subconsciously, she'd kept her apartment for that reason. She'd asked her department chair for an extension of her medical leave. He agreed to hold her position. She didn't have tenure, so she was grateful to him for extending her leave.

In the sitting room, she wrote Leonardo a note and stopped. *For the second time, he chose Caryn over you.* She crumpled up the sheaf of paper and dropped it into the small trash can next to the writing desk.

She thanked his staff for all they'd done and made a special trip to the kitchen to thank Leo's chef for all the great food and special care he provided to her. "I'm sorry to see you go. You and la piquellina Isabella have been a pleasure to cook for. This is for you and Isabella." She hugged him then and left before more tears soaked her face. She didn't know she could produce so many.

She found Nanny B and Izzy waiting in the living room. "The taxi is here, miss. All of our luggage is in the trunk." The puppy was in her carrying case next to Nanny B.

"Are you ready for this fun trip?" she said with false bravado.

"Want Papa." Isabella stomped her tiny foot.

"Oh, we will have an adventure. It will be nice. Just wait and see."

Caryn walked into the living room dressed in a Gucci suit, another pair of stilettos on her feet. She was sure to let Rose see she'd made herself at home. She stood in the center of the living room. Rose said nothing as she held her head up high, and, taking Isabella's hand, Rose squared her shoulders and walked out of Leonardo's villa. Once again, she walked out of his life. This time though, it was his decision. The nanny followed, carrying the dog's case.

Well, he'd said come to recuperate. She did, and now it was time to leave.

Flying home, they were in coach, nothing like flying on his private plane. He didn't even allow them to use one of his helicopters for the trip from Taormina to the airport in Catania. At least they were comfortable in coach on the jumbo jet. Her Italian came in handy, and the flight attendant, seeing how cramped they would be, found an empty row with five seats for them. They could lift the arm rests, and Isabella could lie across two seats. The flight attendant said that it would be all right for the dog to get out of the carrier. They brought her water, and Rose laid one of her training pads on the floor. Then she could put the soiled pad into a plastic disposable bag.

By the time they landed at the international airport in Houston, Texas, she was exhausted. Twenty-one hours of flying from Sicily to Milan, to Texas. Her brain was numb from reliving every moment of their time together. How did she miss the signals? How could she not see through his lies? He was just like his father, and she couldn't fault his nature. She'd never open herself up to this kind of pain again. He'd been honest in his own way, telling her about his father and that he was really very much like him. A womanizing two timer.

When their taxi arrived at her small apartment, Rose lifted a sleeping Isabella into her arms. *OMG, can I carry her without dropping to the ground from exhaustion?* Nanny B said, "Ms. Steele, I'll carry Isabella for you."

Rose nodded. "Thank you." Taking her key out of her purse, she opened the door to her ground-floor, one-bedroom apartment.

"Thank you for helping me. The couch pulls out into a queen-size bed. I keep clean sheets, pillows, and a blanket in the hall closet. In the morning, we can settle up. I don't have any food here… It's late now, so I'll have to get milk and eggs in the morning… also coffee, bread, and butter. It's a short walk to the supermarket."

"You rest, ma'am. It's been an excruciating long trip for you, but now you're home. I will call the nanny agency in the morning and request they prepare my final paycheck from Mr. Vitale. They'll help me secure alternative employment as well."

"I'm glad that the agency will help you. I can certainly

give you a reference and recommendation. I'm sorry about how this turned out. You've been great for Isabella, and I have relied on you. Thank you."

Lady slept on a folded blanket on the floor next to Izzy's bed. Rose climbed into her bed. She was tired and needed to sleep. Tomorrow would be soon enough to pick up the pieces and get her life going again. She hadn't taken the cell phone he'd given her, nor the clothes he bought her. She'd asked Signora Santa Maria to pack only what was hers, none of the clothes Leo had bought for her. "I don't understand. This is not at all like Mr. Vitale."

"That's okay. You can pack all of Izzy's clothes." How would she explain to her daughter?

She rubbed her temples, waiting for the headache to subside. She had some savings and the supplemental pay from her medical insurance was direct deposited into her bank account. She would figure out what to do until January, when the next semester began. She would have to make her savings last until then. *Maybe I can tutor in the meantime.*

CHAPTER 7

*L*eonardo Vitale hurried up the steps of his 747 wide body jet. His pilot and co-pilot stood waiting for him to board. "I want to be in Houston yesterday!"

"Yes, sir, Mr. Vitale. We are cleared for immediate takeoff. The tower is allowing us to skip the line as soon as the door is secured," his pilot said.

"Good." He walked into the cabin, his jaw clenched, his hands making fists. Frank sat in a seat in the lounge area. He glanced up from the papers in his hand as Leonardo passed him. "I'll be in the gym."

After what seemed like an eternity, they landed in Houston. He hadn't calmed down, and now he wanted to pound out his frustration on Rose's front door, but he didn't want to upset Isabella. So instead, he used the door knocker and patiently waited for entry. His jaw had been clenched for most of the trip from Sicily to Houston. Now, he relaxed. The scalding fury in his belly receded.

"What are you doing here? Shouldn't you be on your honeymoon?" Rose snapped.

He didn't miss the hostility in her voice. He should be the angry one, not her. But he didn't have time to answer as Isabella came running towards him. She hugged his leg. "Papa miss you."

He lifted her into his arms. "I missed you too, Princess." Lady came yipping over and scratched at him.

The only one who didn't seem happy to see him was the beauty standing by the front door. Her arms were crossed, and her scowl said it all. Rose's golden hair hung in waves down her back. Her pink mini dress clung to the indent of her waist and the curve of her hips.

Leonardo noticed a slight limp as she favored her good leg. He put Isabella down.

Rose bent to her daughter. "Izzy, will you take Lady and go play in the bedroom for a little while?" she said in a cheery voice.

"Papa come." She pouted. "Want Papa."

"Papa can come in after. Right now, Mommy wants to talk with Papa."

"You go, Princess. I'll be in soon." He kissed her cheek, and then she and the dog ran off to the bedroom.

Leonardo didn't give Rose a chance to speak. He turned to her in exasperation and began, "Imagine my surprise when I found you had gone again. It seems to be your M.O. Pick up and leave when things are not as you would like them to be. At least this time you thought to leave a note. I read the drivel and in my anger, threw it to the floor. 'I don't love you. I've never loved you, and I am taking my daughter and going home. Don't bother to come look for me,' etcetera, etcetera."

"I never wrote those things!"

He failed at keeping the anger from his voice. "I know. I found the second note crumpled in the trash can. I read that one about you're always loving me and how I'll be happier with Caryn... I don't know why or how you thought that.

And then in the middle of all of that, Caryn calls me." He ran his fingers through his hair. "She said she needed to see me. I agreed, and she came to the villa, telling me how she loved me and made a mistake taking my offer. She wants children with me. Imagine that? She wants to start a family." He paced away from Rose and then turned to gaze at her. Her body radiated with anger. Her jaw set, and her lips compressed. "She thought I couldn't see the different handwriting. I was furious with her and told her that if she didn't leave right away, I would have my attorneys nullify our agreement and take everything back. I sent her away."

Rose shrugged a shoulder, keeping her arms crossed over her chest. Her jaw set.

He sighed, huffing out a long breath. "My housekeeper said that Caryn had come to my villa the day you left. That she'd made you cry, although you hid your tears from everyone. I questioned the rest of my staff. My chef is furious with me. Can you believe that? The man had tears in his eyes. I had to listen to him tell me what a fool I am to let you go. It didn't take me long to piece it all together. You left your cell phone and the clothes I had bought you. I found your original note, the one you threw in the trash. The other I know Caryn wrote."

Rose lifted her chin and met his gaze. "I didn't want to cause a scene, and I certainly didn't want to have Isabella upset with Caryn's shouting."

"So, you meekly take her word for everything. Nothing we shared mattered?"

"That's not true. I... I can't do this again. She used my past, Leo. You are the only person I've ever confided in. How could you tell her about the woman who gave birth to me? What she had said to me, not wanting any reminders of my existence."

Rubbing the back of his neck, he winced at the pain in his

gut. "Rose, I never talked with her about your past... The words were unfortunate, but nothing I ever told her. All she knew is we lived together in Naples and that Izzy is my daughter... It's over now. She won't bother us anymore. Please come home with me." His voice meant to seduce her.

He watched as she compressed her lips and shook her head. *So, she's digging her heels in.* Leonardo wanted to kiss the sense out of her. Kiss her and love her until she agreed to anything he wanted. Kiss her into bed, kiss her into marriage. No arguments, no words, no persuasion with anything but his lips all over her lethal body. Kiss her until she would be the one to beg him to marry her—love her, always—the way he wanted to, needed to. Yes, he wanted Rose to tell him how very much she needed him. He would make her see the error of her ways. He would never betray her trust. He loved her beyond all else.

Rose turned away from him, and he knew as she hid her face, she really hid her tears from him. God, he wanted to comfort her. He took a step to close the distance between them and touched her shoulder.

"No! Don't touch me."

He ground his teeth and dropped his hand. "I'm not leaving here without you and my daughter."

She huffed, "I guess you'll have to move here then."

Before he could answer, Isabella called to him. "Papa, play wit me." Lady, with her curly ears bouncing, came running into the living room with Isabella running after her.

"Papa, play peeze," Isabella said. "I miss you." She hugged him.

Rose turned to look at Leonardo. She couldn't go back with him. She stood there in her living room, staring into blue eyes. She loved him; of that she was positive. But to give him all of her. Take a chance with her heart, well, she couldn't.

Isabella pulled on Leonardo's pant leg. "Play wit me an Lady."

"Yes, Princess. Let's go into your room, and we can play with your dolls."

~

THAT'S EXACTLY what it is. I'm afraid of being hurt. He says he loves me and twice he chose Caryn. But did he? Maybe the first time, and that was more because I walked out on him. The second time, she lied, and I allowed her to manipulate me. She played on my vulnerability, and I let her. Never again. I won't let anyone, not even Leo, come between us.

Rose walked into the bedroom and found Leo sitting on the floor holding a teddy bear and talking in a funny voice. "Izzy, do you want tea?"

Isabella held up a pink plastic toy tea cup. "Yes, Mr. Bear, an a biscuit for Lady."

"A treat? We'll have to go to the kitchen and get one."

Isabella jumped up and started toward the bedroom door. "Mama biscuit for Lady."

"Are you and Papa playing tea party?" She gazed at Leo, and her heart was full to bursting for this man who sat on the floor of her one-bedroom apartment in his ten-thousand-dollar custom-made suit, playing with their daughter.

"Yes."

"No running or climbing on the counter. Get Lady her treat, and I will be right in to get you a cookie and some milk."

Leonardo stood up from the floor and placed the stuffed teddy on a chair. Rose walked over to him. "I love you. I love you so very much. So much that I'm scared."

He bent his head to kiss her. "I love you. Ti ammo, mi Amore. Come home with me. Let's put this all behind us."

His lips slid across hers, and she breathed in his delicious scent. He tugged her to him, devouring her mouth with his. They couldn't do much more with their daughter in the kitchen.

"Do you think we could get Nanny Byrd back?"

He glanced at his solid-gold Rolex wristwatch, the one that the king of a Middle Eastern country had presented him with. "Hmm, right about now, she should be boarding my plane."

Rose backed out of his arms. "What? Am I that much of a foregone conclusion?"

"Never, my love, are you predictable. I was prepared to plead and grovel, use any means at my disposal. Including your suggestion to move here. I love you and can't live without you."

"I'll have to pack."

"No, just come away with me."

"But…"

"I will have your apartment packed and everything shipped to Taormina. We will have time on the plane to put any fears you have to rest. We can discuss and plan our future. Right now, I haven't decided how many times I'm going to make you beg me before I make you come… I want to love you all the way home."

"Home. I like the sound of that. I want to raise our daughter in Sicily."

THIS TIME, Rose could walk up the steps of the plane by herself. She held Lady's leash while Leonardo carried Isabella. Once on the plane, Isabella ran right into the arms of her nanny. "Nanny B, yay, you here. We go home."

"Yes, sweetie, we are all going home."

Once everyone was settled, Leonardo sat next to Rose. Isabella, and her nanny, and the puppy sat nearby. The pilot announced they were cleared for takeoff. Nanny Byrd reclined the seats they were in, and Isabella fell asleep cuddled up to her, with Lady curled up next to them.

The wide-body 747 reached cruising altitude, and Leo leaned over to whisper in her ear, "They're sleeping. Why don't we go rest in the bedroom?"

Rose whispered, "I would rather you and I do something perhaps more energetic."

"Ahh, what a great idea." Leonardo stood, and Rose followed as they walked to the master bedroom of Leo's private jet. Leo nodded to one of the flight attendants in the galley.

"Hold lunch for us. I'll ring you when we are ready." His fingers twined with Rose's smaller ones as they proceeded to the bedroom.

He opened the door to the bedroom. The silk shades were drawn down, covering the windows, and the bedroom's muted light was inviting. Leo pulled his tie open and unbuttoned his shirt. Rose went over and turned the bed down.

"Shall we christen this bed?"

"What? You've never taken anyone to bed here? Not even… Caryn."

He snapped his head toward her, and Rose realized that she was wrong to bring up his ex-fiancée. "I'm sorry, Leo, I shouldn't have said that."

"Rose, it's always been you. You are the one I can't live without."

"Leo, I love you so much." She ran her hands into his shirt, touching his skin, rubbing her palms along his pecs and down his abdomen.

Leonardo pulled his shirt apart, and a few buttons scattered on the floor.

"What are you doing?

"Taking you to bed. Lift your arms."

She did, and he grabbed the hem of her mini dress, sliding the fabric over her head. "Better." He pulled her to him, unhooking her pink lace bra. Her blond, silky tresses fell around her, and Leo pushed her hair to one side as he bent to take a nipple into his mouth. He skimmed over her belly and rubbed her mound through her panties.

"Oh, Leo." Rose unbuckled his belt and ran her hand over his groin.

He needed to calm his dick. "Not yet," he breathed, kneeling before her. Sliding the pink panties down her shapely legs, he pressed his lips to her abdomen, spreading kisses lower and lower. Rose's fingers caressed his head, tangling in his hair. Leo held the silken flesh of her buttocks in his hands and pressed her to him. He breathed in her hot, intoxicating scent of desire. He craved her and had to taste her, now, like this. When he loved her with his tongue on her clit like this, she was his. He pressed where he knew she loved to feel him working her bundle of nerves. Her sighs drifted around him.

"Ahh, ahhh, ahhhh, ohh... yes." She trembled, and he stopped. "What?" she groaned. "Don't stop."

He stood, hooking his arm under her knees as he lifted her and walked to the bed. "I'm not finished, Bellissima. You're going to come with my mouth, but I want you to be comfortable."

"Leo... Ohh yes."

The blond curls between her legs glistened, and he stroked her with his finger before parting her wet folds. He sank his tongue into all that delicious heat, and Rose arched into him, giving herself fully to him. He circled her drenched bud before he sheathed his tongue in her over and over. She grasped his hair writhing against his mouth before she cried out. He buried his tongue deep into her as her convulsing waves clenched his tongue. He stroked his finger into her. "No, Leo, I want you. I want your dick in me now."

He slipped out of his pants and boxers, taking a condom from his pocket and rolling it on before he crawled up his beautiful Rose's wanton body. "Yes, my wild Rose."

She cupped his head, lifting herself, reaching her lips to his in a hot open-mouth kiss filled with desire. He thrust into her. "Leo, yes, so good." She wrapped her legs around him, and he thrust into her deeper, faster. "Ooh, ohhh, Leo."

He covered her mouth in an all-consuming kiss, muffling her scream of pleasure as she shuddered and pulsed around him. The tingling began in his lower back, and a fireball of pure bliss that only his wild Rose could elicit from him roared through his body. He exploded in her, gasping for breath.

They lay in each other's arms, covered in a sheen of pleasure. He stroked her hair, the long, silken tresses sliding through his fingers. She sprinkled kisses over his jaw and down his neck. He would never let her go. "Are you hungry?"

"I didn't realize until you asked, but yes, I'm starving. Let's shower and dress, then we can have lunch at the dining table." He called and had everything waiting for them. She hadn't realized the elegance on his plane. Sterling silver place settings gleamed on a white tablecloth. Crystal stemware adorned each china plate. "Are we eating alone?"

"Yes, Frank is entertaining Nanny B with tales of his adventures coming up the ranks from police officer to captain. Isabella is sleeping with Lady snuggled next to her."

A flight attendant served them steak and lobster. He cut into the tender steak. "Why don't you pursue your PhD?"

Rose gazed up from her plate, her eyes round. "Leo, I

would love that." Then she shrugged. "I'm not sure with all the adjustments Izzy will have to make."

"We'll be landing soon. You don't have to decide right this minute. It's an option that you have. I know how important your doctorate was."

CHAPTER 8

ose was back in Taormina, and Leo—true to his word—stayed home more and more. Leonardo bought an office building on the outskirts of Taormina and moved his corporate headquarters from Rome to be closer to home. Joe hired extra staff, two more PAs, and another law firm to handle Vitale Hotels' new acquisitions. More staff for the day-to-day operations was also hired. Frank was happy to settle into his new position as head of the Vitale Hotels' worldwide security division. Leonardo no longer needed an around-the-clock personal bodyguard, which had been his key role. Now in this new position, he got to stay close to Nanny B, or as he called her Byrdie. They'd developed quite a relationship.

Rose loved Leo and wanted to be with him always. She had some amazing news to share with him. How it happened, she wasn't sure. Probably when his condom slipped on Capri; images of them on the round bed with the mirror above flashed through her mind, bringing a smile to her lips.

Twice before, when he was about to ask her to marry

him, it didn't happen. She would be the one to propose—put her heart on the line—this time. She'd planned a surprise for him. Isabella was with Nanny B, so they would have all the privacy they wanted.

She asked Signora Santa Maria to help her prepare a romantic setting for her and Leo. The chef was enlisted to prepare a romantic dinner for them. The housekeeper was so excited to help her.

Now, Rose applied the finishing touches to her makeup while she waited for Leo to come out of the dressing room. She'd chosen a lavender-colored satin slip dress with thin spaghetti straps. The neckline and down the sides of the bodice were trimmed with embroidered lace. The appliques dotted with crystals and beads were hand sewn on to the dress.

She didn't own too much jewelry but on the dressing room vanity, she found the diamond stud earrings that Leonardo had bought her when they were dating, along with a heart-shaped diamond pendant that now lay next to it. She smiled at the flutter she felt in her chest. She put on the earrings and fastened the pendant to her neck.

"You are a vision of beauty." She took in a breath as her lids slid over her eyes. Then she turned, and there was Leo, tall and handsome in a dinner jacket that showed off his broad shoulders and lean waist and pants that accented his long, muscular legs. He would put the statue of Adonis to shame. Leo walked over to her and extended his elbow. "Shall we?"

"Yes," she murmured, taking his arm. He led her to the private patio of the master bedroom, where dinner would be served. The vast darkness of the Ionian Sea stretched below the balcony and the sandy beach etched out onto the coastline. On the patio, two potted palm trees stood in the corner. Their trunks were lit with clear twinkle lights the way they always were in the evening. Rose gasped when she saw the hundreds of tea lights scattered around the patio. Between the flickering candles, the floor was covered with pink rose petals. The housekeeper draped the intimate table in a damask cloth that reached to the stone floor. On the table, the finest china, crystal stemware, and sterling silver place settings gleamed. An ice bucket held sparkling water for her and wine for Leonardo. A bowl filled with flowers and two tapered candles sat in the middle of the table. He pulled an upholstered cathedral-back chair from the table for Rose.

She couldn't wait another minute. Her belly clenched, and she had to ask him right now. She took a deep breath. She held his hand and went down on one knee. "Leonardo Vitale, I love you, and I want to share my life with you. Will you marry me?" He lifted a brow at her before his face split into a brilliant smile. He lifted her into his arms and spun around with her. "Yes, Yes, Yessss."

"Put me down. I'm going to be sick." He stopped, his handsome face showing his concern. He let her feet touch the floor but kept his arms around her waist, steadying her.

"What's wrong? Are you suffering after effects of the concussion?"

The nausea passed as quickly as it began. "How do you feel about being a father again?"

"A baby?" Surprise etched his handsome face.

She nodded and smiled at him. "Now you'll have to marry me."

"Would you like a cool towel?"

"No, I'm better. The queasiness has passed.

Leonardo bent and, holding her to him, pressed kisses over her belly. Then he lifted her into his powerful arms and left the patio to carry her into his study. "What are you doing?"

"You'll see." Then he stood her near his desk.

Leo went to the wall behind his desk and pressed on a set of books lining the shelf. It opened, revealing a safe. His finger moved over the keypad, and the door silently opened. He reached in and removed a small velvet box. He turned and went to stand in front of her. "I have saved this for you since you walked out of the restaurant." He bent down on one knee and opened the lid on the jewelry box. "I accept your proposal, my Bellissima Rose. Si, I will marry you." He held her left hand in his oh so warm hand. "I bought this for you soon after we met." She looked at the antique emerald and diamond ring. A memory of her admiring the exact ring in a jewelry store window when they were in Rome flashed through her mind. It was perfect. A square-cut emerald surrounded by clear diamonds, round and baguette going down the shank. She'd never seen anything as beautiful, and he'd kept it all these years! Tears filled her eyes. He slipped the ring on her finger.

"Leo, I want you so much. I think at times I was so scared that I didn't see clearly. Now I understand that you have always wanted us to share our lives and not just be together. We belong together."

"Yes, my love, always together." She admired the ring he'd saved for her, and then she looped her arms around his neck and tugged him to her so that their lips met in a kiss filled with undying love and promises for the future.

EPILOGUE

October in Sicily, the weather was ideal. The heat of the summer was a distant memory. It was perfect for an outdoor reception. Leonardo wanted to be involved with every step of the wedding planning. In the weeks leading up to their wedding, Rose and Leonardo sat with the head of Vitale Hotels' events coordinator, who introduced them to their wedding planner. Nicole Lago would be exclusive to them for their wedding. She arrived at the villa, sketch pads in hand, taking notes on what they both wanted to incorporate in their wedding before touring the grounds and offering suggestions. "A wide arbor of flowers would be perfect here at the entrance to the garden," she said.

"That will be perfect to set the tone of entering a secret garden." He bent to Rose, brushing his lips over her brow. "What do you think?"

"Yes, Leo, I think it will be beautiful."

Landscapers were hired, and additional plants were ordered. The florist was chosen, the floral decorations for the garden and the cathedral were designed, and flowers were ordered.

Rose and Leonardo were excited to share their day with relatives and friends. They both agreed that Isabella should be included in the ceremony. Rose made an appointment with a top designer, and she and Izzy flew to Milan to meet with him. Isabella was excited about the big party they were going to have. Papa would marry them both.

The designer arrived at the villa two days before the wedding. "I have a shiny sparkly, dress like you, Mama."

"Yes, darling," Rose said, bending to pick up Isabella and hug her. Identical white lace and beaded wedding dresses hung side by side on pearl hangers in the dressing room. Her wedding veil was draped across an accent chair in the dressing room. Leonardo's tux had been moved to his temporary room, down the hall.

Tomorrow, Rose would marry the man she loved. Tonight, she lay in bed naked, tossing and turning. She slipped from the king-size bed in the master bedroom, picked up her gossamer lavender robe, and tied the satin tie around her waist. Barefoot, she tiptoed down the hall to Leonardo's old room. They'd been sleeping together ever since she came back to Taormina almost three months ago. Together, they'd explained to Isabella that mamas and papas slept in the same bed. But tonight—the night before their wedding—Leonardo wanted to follow every tradition, so they would sleep apart. She slowly pressed the lever handle on his door and silently inched the heavy carved-wood door open, peeking her head in not to wake him. The only light in the room came from the moonbeams shining through the open window. She gasped. He was reclining against the headboard, naked. His tall, athletic body silvered in the moonlight. "I miss you," she whispered.

"Amore, I miss you too." He shifted and made room for her on the bed, patting the mattress. She untied her robe and let it slide to the floor, climbing naked onto the bed. "I know it's only one night, but I couldn't sleep without you."

"Come, my wild Rose." She lay in the circle of his muscular arms, her head resting against his broad chest, listening to his sturdy heartbeat. Leonardo stroked her hip, drawing patterns with his finger. "So, you only came here to sleep?"

She squashed the giggle and, taking his hand from her hip, moved it along her lower abdomen, where the new life they created rested. His big hand cradled her abdomen for a moment before she pressed his hand lower over her mound. "What do you think?"

He bent his head, and his tongue traced her lips before he leisurely explored the recesses of her mouth. She needed more from him. Sucking on his tongue, her body pressed against his hand, demanding more. His feather-light touch over her mound wasn't enough. She parted her legs and lifted herself so that his finger slid into her core. *Yes, my love.*

Leonardo broke the kiss and nibbled on her lower lip; at the same time, he slipped a second finger into her.

"Ummm, yes," she moaned as heat uncurled in her belly, lifting her hips. He trailed hot, hungry kisses along her collarbone to the valley of her breasts. Stopping to take a nipple into his mouth, his tongue coaxed the bud into a diamond hard point, before moving to her other breast, treating it to the same lashing of his tongue and draw of his lips. She thrashed her head and clutched him to her. His thumb slid over her clit. "Yes, yes."

He brushed his thumb over her clit again before adding a delicious pressure. She spread her legs, needing him to go deeper. He kissed a trail of fire down from her breasts to her abdomen. He kissed first one inner thigh, and then the other. Her clit cried out for his tongue. Leonardo lifted her leg over his shoulder. He smiled a bone-melting smile at her before he pulled her other leg over his shoulder. "I have you right where I want you, my precious Rose." Taking his thumb from her clit and holding her gaze, he spread her open, and his tongue lashed at her clit.

She writhed against him, lost in pleasure. Leo slipped two fingers back into her core and stroked her deep before he curled them slowly over her g-spot. He kept her at that fever pitch of desire. He knew exactly where and how to lick and suck her until she grew wild in her need, yanking at his thick black hair. She was close… oh… so… close. Her back arched, and her toes curled as pleasure rocketed through her.

"I love you," she panted, holding his head to her. He kissed her center as the last shudders left her sated body. She melted against him as he crawled up her body. Her hands stroked and massaged the muscles of his arms. Reaching up, she pulled his head down to her, kissing him, tasting herself on his tongue. He guided himself to her entrance. She was so ready. "Please, Leo, I need you now."

"Yes, my love." He thrust to the hilt. "Forever begins today, amore mio," he whispered the words in her ear, moving in her before he pulled almost fully out to thrust into her again. "It's our wedding day. I can't wait to see you walk toward me in the cathedral." He lifted her and flipped onto his back. She gasped as he brought her down on his erection. "But right now, I want to watch you come as you ride me."

"Yes, Leo." She lifted herself onto his engorged head. Sliding down his shaft, she thrust her hips forward. Her core quivered and clenched around him as she rocked back. He sat up and kissed her lips, sliding his tongue into her mouth to swirl around hers. She rocked back and forth on him. With his tongue in her mouth, his dick deep in her, he slid his hands to her waist and around to her buttocks, lifting and lowering her on him. She was wild, holding his head, her tongue sparring with his as an orgasm snuck up on her. Whimpering into his mouth, Leonardo moved his hand so that his finger could rub her clit. She screamed her pleasure into his mouth, gyrating on his cock as he excited her clit. She tore her mouth from his, taking in big gulps of air.

"Ahh my wild Rose, do you like my finger sliding on your slippery clit?"

"Yes, so much... I—" Her breath hitched.

"I feel you coming again. I love the way your pussy strokes me and holds me in your wet heat." His words excited her as much as his dick and his finger pressing on her clit. She looped her arms around his shoulders and buried her head in the crook of his neck, kissing him between moans of pleasure as the waves of her orgasm crashed into her. He held her to him, brushing her hair from her face. He kissed her brow. "How is your leg and your arm?"

"Never better. See," she said, lifting herself once more to slide down his shaft.

"Are you ready for more?" he asked, not giving her a chance to answer. He moved her to face away from him. "Spread your knees and rest your head on your arms."

She scrambled to get into one of her favorite positions. "Oh God, Leo, yes." He said nothing, and the anticipation of him taking her like this, she almost came just waiting for him. He stroked her buttocks, and his engorged head rested at her entrance. "Please, Leo." He spread his fingers on her hips, holding her steady, stopping her from moving back to take him into her.

"You have no patience," he said, rubbing the head of his dick around her wet entrance before he plunged into her.

"Yesss, ahh, yes."

"You like that? It's been so long."

He stayed buried deep in her and shifted his hips from side to side. His balls pressed into her wet folds, and she came, holding him in her, muffling her scream of pleasure against her arm. Leo moved in her, pulling out to bury himself to the hilt repeatedly. She listened to his ragged breath and knew he was ready to come. She pushed back against him and tightened her vagina muscles.

"Yes, my wild Rose... just... like... that." Then he buried himself to the hilt, holding her hips steady. He groaned, and she felt him erupt, shooting his hot seed into her. She loved the feel of him coming in her. She couldn't hold back, and she came again. He fell forward on her panting and then rolled with her to lie on the bed. Covered in a sheen of perspiration, he kissed her behind her ear. "I can't wait until tonight when I will make love to you all night long as Mrs. Vitale."

TODAY WAS A PICTURE-PERFECT DAY, with a cloudless blue sky. It was her wedding day. Luckily, she wasn't showing yet. Soon enough, everyone would know that she and Leonardo were adding to their family.

Leonardo's grandmother and all his friends would be at the church. Rose's friends from the university in Texas and her co-workers from the archaeology unit here in Italy would also be there, as well as the director of the Pompeii dig and so many more. Her nurse, Ms. Carrington, from when she recuperated here in Sicily was also slated to attend. They would all be at the cathedral for the wedding and then at the intimate reception held in the villa's garden.

Days had been spent decorating the garden. The arbor of fresh flowers leading to the garden was anchored in place.

Lights were added to the palm tree trunks, and more lights were strung through the bushes. Ropes made of fresh flowers were brought in and hung from the tree branches. The flower beds were all filled with fragrant, fresh flowers. Pink and white roses lined one side of the garden. Rows of tables were set up and decorated with white tablecloths that puddled to the floor. Gold spindle-back chairs were set up at each place setting. Tall, gold pedestal candelabras lined the tables, interspersed with matching lower ones. In each clear glass globe, a white candle sat. They would all be lit just before the guests arrived back from the cathedral. To one side, close to the edge of the garden, a dance floor was set up and beyond, a view of the sea.

The chef insisted on making the wedding dinner for all the guests, hiring extra staff to prepare and serve the formal wedding feast. Leonardo, with all his elegant hotels around the world, was happy when Rose chose an intimate setting in Taormina. The chef brought in his brother, who was a pastry chef, to make the wedding cake. The beauty of Sicily shone this day. Isabella and her nanny would stay with Leo's grandmother for two weeks while they went on a honeymoon.

Rose's heart pounded an excited beat as she lifted her bridal bouquet, pressing her face into the arrangement and inhaling the delicate scent of fresh roses. White velvety smooth roses, baby's breath, and myrtle were held together with a white satin ribbon. Their names and today's date were written in gold across the ribbon.

Rose placed a crown of delicate baby's breath intertwined with pink and white rosebuds on Isabella's head. "You look so pretty, my beautiful Izzy," she said as she hugged her.

Leonardo had bought her a diamond tiara to attach to her veil. Once the hairdresser left, Joan, her maid of honor, helped her attach the cathedral-length veil. Her wedding dress had a train, but the veil would extend past the end of that. She was having a dream wedding because she was marrying her dream guy.

She fluffed Isabella's dress, took a breath, and turned to Joan. "Thank you for helping today." Then she smoothed her dress, and it was time to get in the limousine for the drive to the cathedral. A floral archway of pink and white roses, jasmine, sweet pea, and ivory framed the open doors of the cathedral. Tall standing arrangements of the same flowers lined the entry through to the aisle. A white runner ran down to the altar where Leonardo waited with the Cardinal and his best man, his cousin on his mother's side. Each pew on both sides of the aisle was decorated with the same flowers. Joan helped her arrange her train and veil. Then she went to stand in front of her and Isabella.

Joan whispered, "It looks so beautiful, and the fragrance from all these flowers is fabulous." She held a basket of pink and white rose petals to scatter on the runner as they walked to the altar.

"Mama pretty princess."

"Just like you, darling. Are you ready to walk with me to Papa?"

"I ready." Rose smiled. Her daughter looked beautiful. She carried a heart-shaped wreath in the same design as the crown of flowers in her hair. Joan took her place at the altar, and then the bridal march began. Rose took a deep breath as the guests stood, and all eyes were on her and Izzy. Having no parent, she chose to walk alone with Isabella and the new baby whose heart beat under her breast to the man she loved. Everything was so perfect and right. Their lovemaking last night was magnificent. She found Leonardo's gaze, and the world melted away. Only he mattered as she walked toward the only man she'd ever loved. His whispered words from last night filled her head. "Forever begins today, my love." He slid a diamond eternity band on her finger, and she, with trembling fingers, placed a gold band on his finger.

I HOPE you enjoyed Rose and Leonardo's story.

ALSO BY CINDY REDDING

The DiMarco Empire Series
The Sicilian's Betrayal
The Winemaker's Seduction
The Frenchman's Revenge
The Sea Captain's Redemption

Christmas
A Fake Date for Kate

The Royals
A Royal Temptation

More Romances
The Tycoon's Secret Child

WHERE TO FIND MY BOOKS

You can find my books at your favorite bookstore, retailer, or library 

Or, you can buy them directly from me at my website https:// CindyReddingAuthor.com

Or,

Cindy's Store https://payhip.com/CindyRedding

If you prefer, please scan this QR Code with your phone

ABOUT THE AUTHOR

USA TODAY Bestselling Author **Cindy Redding** writes what she loves. Contemporary sizzling hot and spicy romance. Inspired by her travels around the world and her love of Italy, Cindy's romances come alive with hot-blooded men and strong-willed independent women. Escape to a world where happily ever after lives.